The Last Day at Bowen's Court

A NOVEL

The Last Day at Bowen's Court

A NOVEL

Eibhear Walshe

SOMERVILLE PRESS

Somerville Press Ltd,
Dromore, Bantry,
Co. Cork, Ireland

©Eibhear Walshe 2020

First published 2020

This book is a work of fiction and except in the case of historical fact, any resemblance to actual persons, living or dead, is purely coincidental.

Designed by Jane Stark
Typeset in Adobe Garamond Pro
seamistgraphics@gmail.com

ISBN: 978 1 999997083

Printed and bound in Spain
by GraphyCems, Villatuerta, Navarra

For Rory O'Boyle

Historical Note

In this novel, I have created a fictional version of the interconnected lives of Elizabeth Bowen, Charles Ritchie, and of Bowen's husband Alan Cameron and Ritchie's wife Sylvia Ritchie, all of them real people. Throughout the novel, I've invented conversations, letters and events and I have drawn liberally on Bowen's own fictions to do so. These four people existed, though perhaps not as I portray them, but all of the other characters in this novel are my invention.

Acknowledgements

It was a pleasure to live through the writing of this novel and my admiration for Elizabeth Bowen and my love for her work grew stronger as I wrote and so I offer my version of her life as a tribute and a homage. I want to thank Marina Carr for generously sharing her play on Bowen with me. I am greatly indebted to the fine Bowen scholar Heather Corbally Bryant, for her dear friendship and for her insightful and inspiring reading of the manuscript. Other Bowen scholars like Allan Hepburn, Victoria Glendinning, Nick Turner and the *Bowen Review*, Mike Waldron, Keri Walsh, Derek Hand, and Flicka Small were of so much help and I would also like to thank Sally Phipps for reading the novel and for her kindness in sharing her loving memories of Bowen. Virginia Brownlow, Claire Connolly, Oonagh Cooney, Madeleine Darcy, Éilis ní Dhuibhne, Noreen Doody, Anne Fitzgerald, Lee Jenkins, Dermot and Ann Keogh, Ann Luttrell, Danielle McLaughlin, Mary O'Donnell, Eimear O'Herlihy, Ladette Randolph, Ciaran Wallace, Ria White, thanks to you all for all your support and friendship.

This novel was researched amongst the Bowen papers at the Harry Ransom Center and I would like to thank the staff and the Director, Stephen Ennis for all his help. It was written at the Centre Cultural Irlandais and revised at the Cité Internationale des

Arts, Paris and I want to thank Nora Hickey M'Sichili at the CCI, and the staff of both wonderful institutions for making me feel so welcome. I received a Cork City Council Arts Bursary, and an Arts Council Travel Bursary and UCC, CACSSS publication and travel grants, and UCC School of English travel grants to work on the book and I am very grateful for all of this practical help.

I want to thank my mother Celine Walshe, for her unwavering support and love. As always, Donald O'Driscoll was the first reader and his belief in my version of the story of Bowen and Ritchie was crucial to the writing and made the novel happen for me. I am very grateful to my partner Saul Perez for his generous help and interest and for believing in me.

Great thanks are due again to Andrew and Jane Russell at Somerville Press and to my agent Christopher Sinclair Stevenson.

I dedicate this novel to my dear friend, Rory O'Boyle, who accompanied me all through the writing and thank him for our wonderful friendship.

Elizabeth! I woke at four this morning, calling your name, shouting it out to the empty bedroom. You had just left, or so it seemed to me, your presence in the dark room still palpable, your departing spirit waking me up. Such cruelty to leave me in this hollowed out place. I sat up, fully awake, despite all the whiskey and I thought… 'So. I'm still alive?' I wonder if I should feel grateful. Now I lie here and watch the first touch of light creep along the edge of the curtains and wonder why I am not dead yet, like you, dead all these years now. It seems impossible that you are dead twenty years. It seems to me you just left this room, staying a moment to wake me up and then abandon me. All I want to do is dream of you again while I lie here and wait for the dawn. My dream. It's very simple. The roses in Regent's Park, a summer's day, you lying on the grass, elegant, smoking gracefully, telling me about your latest book. My dream of you. Of us.

I had another dream last week. Rows of your books, on a shelf before me. I stood before them, thinking…Elizabeth. Bitha. If I read them all, would I find you? Are you hidden there? Or are the books themselves unravelling? Was I the flaw in your story? You were always stronger than me. The cruel strength of the writer. Telling our story. Our dream of each other. My dream of you. The last day at Bowen's Court, although we didn't know it was the last day.

1941

The first February of the war. The beginning of their siren years. Unexpectedly, he became her lover when London was in peril and at a time when Elizabeth felt as if she were moments away from random, senseless obliteration. Knowing this, falling in love with Charles all through the spring and summer of 1941, she knew fear and excitement in equal measure, saw nothing but his slender face and hands, and heard only his voice, felt the touch of his mouth on hers. In the most terrifying time of her life, wondering if each morning at her typewriter would be her last, she found an excitement she learned to love.

She remembers the moment when she first saw him. It was during the christening. He was sitting ahead of her in the church and it was his dark hair and his neck that first drew her attention to him. Sitting there, she began to imagine touching that neck, feeling the strong tendons, the warm skin under her caressing fingers. It was only when Alan jabbed her with his elbow did she come to her senses and stand up. Afterwards, standing on the church porch, the tall young man in the dark suit glanced at her and then, after a moment, lost interest and turned away elsewhere. She told herself, with determination that if she had her chance, someday this young man would not turn away from her.

At the house party, she had wandered upstairs, with her drink in her hand, to look towards Romney Marsh. In the chilly library on the first floor, she stood at the full-length window, watching the light begin to fade on the misty Kentish landscape, a landscape familiar from her childhood. After a few minutes, she heard someone walk into the room behind her, the soft tread of footsteps on the wooden floor. She stood where she was, without turning around, hoping it was the unknown young man from the church porch. It was. He came to stand behind her. Silence and then a few moments later,

'So? What exactly are we looking at?'

His voice for the first time, deep and caressing, almost in her ear.

'Romney…m…m…Marsh away to the west, where the sun is setting.' She managed without too much stammering.

Another silence. She dared not turn. The sound of chatter from downstairs. In the far distance, the early glow of red intensifying over the marsh, as if a fire was creeping towards them.

'Glorious.'

'England at its best.'

'Spoken like a true Englishwoman.'

She turned to face him, looking up into his face, his eyes warm, gleaming behind his glasses.

'Except, I'm Irish.'

She smiles to banish any reproach. He looks amused.

'I never would have guessed.'

'You English always make that sound like a compliment. I'm not quite sure why.'

'Except… I'm Canadian. Charles Ritchie.'

'Elizabeth Cameron.'

Standing looking directly into each other's eyes, she prays no one comes and disturbs them. Alan has a bad habit of following her around at this time of day, anxious to go home. The glass behind her rattles slightly in the breeze of early evening. She can hear her name

1941

being called from below. Alan.

'Bitha!'

'That's for me. Bitha. Elizabeth. Can we offer you a lift back to London?'

'I'm staying.'

He stands to one side to let her past. She cannot quite go, not with that look in his eyes, holding her there.

'Come for a drink sometime. 3 Clarence Terrace. By Regent's Park. Fridays are best. After 6.'

'3 Clarence Terrace,' he says nodding. 'I will.'

'Alan keeps us supplied with unpatriotic amounts of decent sherry. I'm not quite sure where he gets it. Best not to inquire too closely.' Best to get Alan's name out there as soon as possible.

'Perhaps he spies?'

Alan now on the stairs below. Calling more urgently.

'Bitha!'

'Fridays at 6. Spying, that's my job, actually.'

'3 Clarence Terrace,' he replies.

The next day Elizabeth phoned her cousin Angela who seemed to know him at the christening.

'Yes, charming isn't he. Not exactly handsome and yet. At the Canadian Embassy. Knows all the right people. There is, or was, a tall girl. Eva. American. Heiress of some kind. It's like a Henry James novel. Nobody knows if she is his girlfriend anymore.'

When he finally called for sherry at Clarence Terrace, Elizabeth brought him in to meet Alan.

'Alan, have you met my pal from the Canadian Embassy?'

Charles looked all around the room and then glanced out onto the park. Alan nodded approvingly as he pours him a sherry.

'Best view in London. You won't get that in Canada House.'

Charles turned towards Elizabeth.

'I feel as if I've been here already. Thanks to your book.'

He has a copy of her last novel.

'You never told me you are Elizabeth Bowen. The Elizabeth Bowen.'

Elizabeth laughed.

'I suppose, I am. Amongst other things. Be careful, you may end up in my next book.'

Alan handed Charles a sherry, adding a little boastfully.

'I've warned Bitha, if I ever end up in one of her productions, then I'll clear out.'

Elizabeth fixed Alan with a steady gaze.

'Alan, I can keep Charles company. Your committee is at seven.'

At this, Alan looked a little startled. After Alan leaves, Charles sits down opposite her and asks.

'So? Tell me all about your spying.'

And she did.

The following day, as she sat at her desk, thinking about Charles, roses arrived, with a card, asking her to lunch. After lunch, he decided to delay his return to the office and they walked for an hour after lunch in the park in the cold March air. On the way home, she began to wonder at the giddy happiness that had suddenly landed on her. During the evening, sitting reading, with Alan at his household accounts across the fire from her, she found herself saying his name again and again, wordlessly.

Charles phoned her late one evening the following week, her first time hearing his voice on the phone. It is deep, calm, with a touch of Canada around the edges of his clipped, careful tones. He sounded a little urgent. He had just read another of her novels and was full of questions about it. Was she free to talk now? Alan was standing nearby, holding her coat in a pointed manner. No, she had a dinner

1941

appointment that evening. They must meet. Was she free that following afternoon for tea? She was.

At tea, Charles began his interrogation of her.

'But your home, Alan, everything, yourself. You put them all in. How can you do that? What does he say?'

She shrugged and changed the subject. Alan was not to be discussed between then. She stared at him intently for a few moments, narrowing her eyes and then laughed.

'I should like to put you in my next novel.'

He flushed and looked pleased and they walked out into the fine evening light. Looking at the searchlights above her, for the first time, she began to worry about being killed.

As the evenings lengthened, he began to phone her in the early evenings, coming to dinner whenever she asked him, becoming very popular with her friends, who began to include him in invitations to cocktails in their apartments. Always, when she was thinking about him, a letter or a card arrived, asking her to meet him. A vista was gradually opening out on a miraculous new territory. In this new country, she walked with a confident step, assured of the firm ground underneath.

A warm day in April and they linger in Regent's Park, Elizabeth lying down in the sun, her raincoat beneath her, telling him about her new novel.

'This moment. London. Now. That's what I am after.' And you, she says to herself.

At lunch the next day, she told him about her current war reporting. He looked worried and told her to be careful where she spoke about it.

'Certainly not in Ireland, if I were you. They might not understand in Dublin. I can't answer for County Cork, never having been there.'

'We must remedy that,' she told him and he looked pleased.

'I'd like that. I want to see Danielstown for myself.'

All during that time, at breakfast, making coffee for Alan, reading letters, she was seeing each new day in the light of Charles' being in existence. With her papers before her, she sat at the desk every morning. Instead of writing, she would interrogate herself. Did she desire him? She was unsure. Was she in love with him? Emphatically. Did he feel the same? She couldn't guess and preferred not to know. By all evidence, he was clearly drawn to her but was it because she was a writer. When they met, it was for lunch, or in the evenings with others but never alone. She had made it clear that Alan need never be invited and was beginning to wonder if she needed to make other things clear to Charles as well.

In the afternoons, her writing done, she stood in the window overlooking the park, and told herself, 'I can live in these two worlds. I can. I can endure the everyday world while counting the minutes until I can escape to the other, the dream world.'

Once, staring out of her window, waiting for Charles to call in for a drink, she turned to find Alan looking at her.

'The park's closed again,' she told him. 'Another unexploded bomb.'

Alan said nothing, continuing to look at her and then turned abruptly to leave. She shrugged, unwilling to think about the look in Alan's eyes as he had stared at her.

There were dark moments, when she was convinced she was deluding herself and feeling her age, the gap of seven years, and the thought of younger prettier women. She wondered about Eva and even asked Angela, her source of gossip from the Canadian Embassy if she knew anything about her.

'Not a whisper but leave it to me,' she promised. Later that week, at a cocktail party, to Elizabeth's horror, Angela tackled Charles directly.

'And how is that charming American girl, you know, the tall one? Oh, my silly head and names!'

1941

Charles smiled down at her, unwilling to help her.

'You know. Eva, isn't it? Do you hear anything of her these days?'

'Gone over to Belfast on some mission, I believe. I'm not terribly sure.'

He answered calmly but Elizabeth, listening with every nerve straining, was not at all sure herself.

In late April, with a sudden feeling of imminent resolution hanging in the air, she was walking past the National Gallery, glorying in the endless light of the bright early summer evening when she heard her name being called.

It was Charles, in a taxi. He waved at her to stop and got out.

'What good luck? I've finished early today and was going to call into Clarence Terrace. Time for a drink?'

He got out and they strolled together up Pall Mall, silent for once. Usually they could talk for hours, but, this unexpected meeting, the bright sunlight of the evening, the glances that they darted covertly at each other, all made this new territory. They found somewhere for a drink, and, after some hesitation, he suggested staying on for dinner. At one point she phoned the flat, to discover Alan had returned from work and told him she might stay in Angela's that evening, she wasn't sure. He told her crisply to enjoy herself but hung up before she could say good night.

When she got back to the table, Charles told her about a small night club, nearby, in Baker Street, where he sometimes went to drink in the evenings and they walked there. Now, conspicuously alone together, this made her even more tongue-tied as they drank vermouth and listened to the band.

A loud table of ten or so people in full evening dress sat right next to them. In their midst, a woman, near her own age, with pale blond hair and a worn look, sat with a small fox fur slung around her shoulders. As the evening progressed, she realised that the woman kept looking at them. Finally, she mentioned it to Charles.

'Charles, I do believe that we are under surveillance.'

He glanced around and caught the eye of the woman, sitting at the edge of the large party, their table right next to them. She was expensively made up, with an unfinished drink before her. Her companions were talking around her, but nobody seemed to be talking to her. She kept drawing on and off her ocelot gloves. As she did, she glared over at Charles.

He shrugged and turned back to Elizabeth. An unpleasant thought crossed her mind. A spurned lover. Her future perhaps.

'Do you know her?'

'Never saw her before in my life.'

As they chatted, the party across from them began standing up, somewhat to her relief, as the malign glances of the woman had become more and more overt. The woman started gathered up her gloves and her bag, tugging her fox fur more tightly around her. Then, swaying slightly on her feet, she walked towards them. Charles looked up but stayed sitting where he was.

'I just want to say, young man,' she began, in a soft, whispery kind of voice, her face hesitant, somehow unfocussed, 'that you should be ashamed of yourself not to be in uniform …'

She stopped. Her hair, expensively peroxided, seemed to quench her pale face and make her seem transparent. Charles sat impassively, staring up at her. The woman shook off the arm of an older man who had come up behind her and was attempting to draw her away. Charles sat smoking, his eyes fixed on the woman, his gaze unruffled. The woman turned towards Elizabeth. A look of real venom came across her face, tightening her mouth, her real prey in sight.

'And, as for you, at your age....'

1941

Charles cut across her, quietly, sharply.

'You are disturbing us.'

Charles looked up at the woman and she stopped. Elizabeth wondered the woman could stand there so calmly, his long, handsome face now transformed by a forbidding look that froze off all further conversation from her by force of expression. Why was the woman not more afraid?

He turned back to Elizabeth and asked,

'Another drink, darling?'

The woman in the fox fur looked as if she was going to strike him. He stood up, very quickly and faced her from his greater height and she stumbled back a step, her companion using the opportunity to take her arm and draw her away.

Charles turned to the waiter.

'Two more vermouth cocktails, please.'

They drank in silence, both unwilling to discuss the unwelcome attentions of the woman. Darling. He had never called her that before.

'You know,' she remarked, more for something to say, 'That was unpleasant but, these days, I always feel that there is a third always at our table.'

Charles looked at her quizzically.

'You mean Alan?'

'Well, no actually. I meant the war.'

She paused and decided to be blunt.

'You know, as far as that goes, Alan and I go our separate ways. Always have.'

He nodded.

'I presumed so.'

He stood up.

'It is getting late. I'll fetch you a taxi.'

She stayed sitting. So this was it. She had made it as clear as possible and he wanted to leave. Something wintry growing within her chest made her want to sit and stay where she was.

'I don't want to go home. You go if you like.'

He stared at her, and, for a moment, she thought, break my heart but don't waste my time.

Instead he took her hand and drew her to her feet. Outside the night had crept up on them, blazing with an intense moonlight, Baker Street brilliantly illuminated, making a mockery of the shuttered and darkened windows around them. He took her hand again and kept it firmly within his.

'Where to?' he asked.

She thought.

'Not Clarence Terrace.'

'And not my place,' he added, too. 'My cousin Sylvia is staying.'

They walked on into the evening, London flooded with moonlight, the skies above them peaceful, and the illusion of safety in the clear night. As they walk towards Regent's Park, the full moon glares down on the deserted street, making the walls of the buildings around them glitter as if made of sand. It is just midnight, the buses have already stopped and it is if they are alone in the London night. The sky above them, without any clouds, seems endless and vulnerable, the city more nakedly defenceless than she cares to think of. She shudders to think that she and Charles and all of them are clearly visible to any plane above them. Their faces pale in the remorseless light, they turn to face one another, her hand kept firmly within his. The warm grip, longed for in the months of their turning towards each other, was like the feeling of sun, this night now made into ghostly day again.

'Where to?' he asks.

She thought.

1941

'Not home. Alan is there, and Angela is staying. Too crowded.'
She feels awkward in saying this, cursing their bad luck.
'Your place?'
'I'm not quite sure,' he tells her. 'Let me phone.'
He keeps her hand firmly in his and they walk onwards towards Regent's Park in search of a phone box. To the side of them, through the trees, they catch glimpses of the lake glittering like silver through the gateway, now stripped of its iron gates. Ahead of them, two soldiers stand watching the ducks flying about unhappily in this ghostly version of daylight. The men, young, French by the sound of their voices, seem a little drunk, swaying as they stand there, clinging on to each other for support, laughing every time the ducks flap and splash in the water. Elizabeth and Charles walk beyond them, and stop to observe the familiar terrain of the park, made unfamiliar by the late hour and the deserted pathways.

Anxious to prolong these moments with him alone, she tells him.
'Let's go in, shall we? I've never been in the park in moonlight.'
He hesitates but she drops his hand and strides onwards, his steps behind her, into the familiar made into a new world. They circle the lake, the shimmering silver fragmented and broken by the fuss of the ducks but she walks them over to the far side, where the water is undisturbed and the flat sheet of water reflects a perfect, almost terrifying moon and their own silhouette, dark, sinister, flattened.

They stand there for a few minutes, the rose bushes blanched of habitual colour in this merciless light, all the colours now fugitive and something of the eternal seems to her to have invested itself into the landscape of this night-time city. Charles takes her hand and kisses it and the ghostly light makes her think of a few lines of verse from her childhood. Touching his arm, she says, 'Mysterious Kor'.

'What?' he asks her, smiling. Just behind them, through the railings on the street, the French soldiers have begun some loud, unmelodic singing, upsetting the wild fowl, who fuss and splash their way towards the French soldiers. This sudden violence shatters the perfect moon at their feet and, their damage done, the two young men march off arm in arm towards a group gathered outside a nightclub. She stops to look across at the deserted street, the houses caught in the glare of the moon, made ancient and uninhabited by the night. The Victorian turrets on one of the buildings have been transformed into a grey fortress in the light, the ruddy colours all drained away.

She struggles to remember and then it comes back to her.

'"Mysterious Kor", thy walls forsaken stand, thy lonely towers beneath a lonely moon.'

He turns and smiles.

'God, I haven't heard that since I was a child. "Mysterious Kor." So much indecent obsession.'

'I think it was the first book I read that really explained obsession to me.'

'Did you read it much?'

'All the time. I always wanted to see the city. "Mysterious Kor". I knew it would be perfect. The abiding city.'

He looks around him, the trees swaying slightly in the breeze, the pungent scents of the undergrowth in full night release and he nods.

'We have it. Here. And we are the last two alive on earth. Time to repopulate it.'

He turns and takes her in his arms and kisses her. Long awaited, she leans into him, his tall lean frame surprisingly solid and firm. She breaks from him and stands back to touch his face, the face she has been dreaming of, touching its long, beautiful lines with her finger for the first time, growing accustomed to its nearness, its shape. She takes off his glasses gently. His face looks more vulnerable, younger, unbearably soft and tender. He draws her into his body again and she burrows against him.

'God, we need to get to a bed.'

She takes his face back into her hands and kisses him again with more passion, pushing his teeth open with her tongue and finding his. Here in the park, where she walks most days, and where it is almost part of herself, this night-time world has become a midnight Eden, ghostly, uncanny, theirs alone. She was reluctant, almost superstitiously afraid to go, to break the spell. But Charles takes her by the hand and they walk slowly back out of the park and into the streets. Outside, they pause to kiss again, more urgently. The rattle of a car moving slowly past makes them spring apart, wartime noises more deadly than those before, and he takes her hand and walks her along the street to a phone-box at the corner. Still holding her hand, he brings her into the phone-box and dials the number. The proximity is pleasant, the sense of being shut in with him and he smiles down at her. He looks down at his tie.

'Time to retire this, I think? Sylvia? Charles here. Sorry if I got you up, old girl. Yes, I know, way past midnight. Look here, is Aunty still with you?'

From behind his back, she can hear a tiny voice, gentle and clear. Charles smiles at her, nods then answers.

'Safely dispatched to Liverpool, is she? And you?'

Again the tiny voice. Elizabeth reaches over to adjust his tie, which has gone awry and he takes her hand and kisses it.

'Poor you. Up at dawn. O.K., we will be there in about half an hour. Put on the kettle, there's a good girl.'

He hangs up.

'We are in luck. Aunty took the last train to Liverpool and Sylvia follows her first thing in the morning. You can bunk in with Sylvia for the night and then we have the place to ourselves from dawn.'

Charles' new flat, the result of his promotion, is at the top of a tall house near Whitehall. At the top of several flights of stairs, he pauses at a door to fumble with his key while she waits behind him. Pushing open the door, he calls, 'Halloo'. From inside, a quiet voice answers 'Halloo' and Charles leads Elizabeth into the small kitchen. There standing over a stove, stirring a pan of milk is a young girl in a cretonne housecoat, her hair bound into braids like a coronet around her head. On the kitchen table is a tin of drinking chocolate and three mugs. The girl turns around and Elizabeth can see that she is not a girl but a woman in her early thirties, blond, fair-skinned, petite. She smiles and holds out her hand.

'I'm Sylvia.'

Just as Elizabeth is about to introduce herself, Charles looks down at the cups.

'Drinking chocolate! Just the ticket. Clever Sylvia.'

His cousin laughs quietly and darts a glance at Elizabeth.

'He calls me the commendable one. You know, after the song. Who is Sylvia, where is she.'

Elizabeth finishes it for her.

'That all her swains commend her. Yes indeed. Drinking chocolate, I haven't had that since the war started.'

'I brought it from Canada. Charles and his sweet tooth.'

There is something very sweet about this girl and she smiles very shyly. Elizabeth is about to introduce herself when Charles picks up a book from the kitchen table and strikes Sylvia playfully on the shoulder with it.

'You've been pilfering from my Library again, Syl. Don't dare take this with you on the train tomorrow, do you hear me, you sly baggage.'

Elizabeth looks. It is the copy of her novel that she had given Charles, *The House in Paris*. Inscribed. She most certainly cannot take it, Elizabeth thinks.

1941

Sylvia pours out the hot milk into the cups with practised ease and looks over.

'Oh please Charles, let me borrow it. I want to know what happens to the child Leopold. Does he meet his mother?'

Turning to Elizabeth, Sylvia offers her a cup, which she takes gratefully.

'Have you read it? It starts slow but is gripping. Charles knows her, you know. Elizabeth Bowen. Or Mrs Cameron, as you have to call her. Very famous. She sounds a little scary.'

Charles has been attempting to cut her off but fails and now Elizabeth laughs gently, then realises who Sylvia thinks she is. Eva. She grows angry but keeps the anger from her voice as much as she can.

'I am she. But please call me Elizabeth. Am I really scary, Charles?'

Sylvia looks confused and Charles stands there, saying nothing so, picking up her cup, Sylvia says she needs to finish her packing and flees the kitchen. As soon as she is gone, Elizabeth turns to Charles and with a deliberately light tone, asks.

'So she was expecting Eva, was she?'

Charles makes a dismissive gesture with his hand.

'Eva is ....'

He pauses and she tries desperately not to show how anxious she is to know exactly what Eva is to him.

'Yes? What is Eva? We never talk about her, Charles.'

'We, she and I. Well there's very little to it, to tell the truth.'

'Tell me about that very little.'

Just then Sylvia comes back into the kitchen with a bundle of blankets.

'Right, I must get some sleep, my train is at an ungodly hour. I'll camp out on the sofa.'

'No need, Syl, you and Elizabeth can have my room and I'll take the sofa.'

The Last Day at Bowen's Court

Charles' bed lies along the wall under the window and Elizabeth wonders about sleeping so close under glass but Sylvia has already gone to sleep on the far side, by the wall curled up with a pillow in her arms. Elizabeth undresses quickly and gets into bed. Her movement disturbs the curtain and a beam of powerful silver light falls across the bed, keeping her awake. She wonders if she should have phoned Alan. She feels sure he will guess. She glances at Sylvia next to her and thinks, 'I will never get to sleep here.'

She slips out of the bed and goes out to look out the window at the houses opposite, the white light beaming down on her. On the huge Victorian mantelpiece Charles' brushes and a stack of ties left carelessly on the back of a chair, his coat hanging on a rack. A shirt lies on the back of a chair, a blue striped one she has seen him wear. Glancing over at the girl sleeping in the bed, she takes the shirt in her hands and then tentatively puts it to her face. She gets back into bed, and is eventually lulled to sleep by the calm sound of Sylvia's breathing.

At four, the sound of a church bell wakes her and the slight warmth from the body next to her makes her move closer. In doing so, she disturbs Sylvia, who flings out one hand, its back knocking Elizabeth lightly across the face. The slap, unconscious, shocks Elizabeth and unexpectedly she finds herself becoming a little tearful. The nightmarish glare of the moonlight, the deathly quiet of the deepest moment of the night. She thinks about getting up and fleeing the bed and making her way home. Charles is asleep in the sitting room. She could make her way out through the kitchen without disturbing him but she hesitates. She sits up and asks herself.

'What am I doing here, in a strange bed, waiting for a man to join me in the morning, with my house and my husband a mile or so away?'

Something makes her stay where she is. The spell of the midnight Eden, the park made eternal by moonlight, Charles and herself standing

1941

there. The force of this spell begins to frighten her. She wonders if she is powerless to leave this room. She lies back and waits for sleep and dreams fitfully, of attacks and of fleeing through a deserted city, of the glass from the window falling over her like a deadly shower of bridal confetti. The memory of that unconscious slap stays with her. Dimly conscious of Sylvia rising a few hours later, Elizabeth buries her head mulishly in her pillow, refusing to say good bye. She can hear the quiet murmur of voices in the other room between Charles and Sylvia and then finds herself in a deep sleep again.

Elizabeth awakes feeling someone is watching her in the morning when she wakes up, Sylvia is gone and Charles is standing there undressing. She watches as he unbuttons the night shirt, and seeing his body for the first time, looks at his lean chest, the strong arms, and the dark hair on his chest. He steps out of his pyjamas and moves towards her, taking her in his arms and she lies back to contemplate his face above hers, still, unable to move.

Hythe
1942

Charles catches his first glimpse of Elizabeth. Something makes him pause, although their train is due to leave within the next few minutes. She is below him in the busy concourse of St Pancras, standing alone in a shaft of early morning sunlight. He looks from the balcony and marvels at her calm self-possession, her case at her side, her gloves held firmly in her hands. On her lapel, she wears a large glass brooch and, as she moves to put down her handbag, it glitters and winks momentarily in reflected sunlight. He stays where he is, the thought of their weekend pressing down on him unpleasantly. What if their train gets hit by a bomb? Or the quiet hotel in Hythe suddenly torn apart. All their careful planning and discretion, undone in a random attack.

Across the concourse, above the noise of the station, the large clock moves towards the hour and still he stays where he is. Four months ago, he first glimpsed her, a stranger, standing in a church porch, lighting her cigarette. He could see then, as he watched her, that she was perfectly aware of his glance, fully in possession of herself. And now they were travelling to Hythe to spend a night together, their status as lovers now in the open, at least to each other. And, in some

Hythe 1942

way, known to her husband, or so he presumed.

But now, standing in the station, delaying his encounter with her, all the days and weeks since their first meeting seem to have vanished. Now the woman waiting for him is as much a stranger to him as on the first day he saw her. And so he watches, marvelling at her apparent calm.

As he stands there, she stoops to push her handbag next to her small suitcase, rescuing it from an approaching crocodile of school children, probably being evacuated to the country, he thinks. Each child wears a large brown label pinned on their dark gabardine coats like parcels. In a sudden lunge, one little girl breaks rank to stamp her foot at a pigeon, the bird rearing up in a flurry of outrage and flying towards the sun. She is firmly dragged back into line by a bossy looking woman. The thought crosses his mind. They could all be dead, those precious children, in a moment. That independent girl, the pigeon bleeding at her feet, the child's future cruelly ended here and now. The thought wakens him from his reverie and he makes his way downstairs.

'Nearly late, nearly late,' he mutters as he hurries towards her. She turns to smile at him.

'Charles,' she says, her voice soft, pleased, surprised almost.

She looks like someone in a dream, her eyes slightly unfocussed. The dazzling sunlight around her blurs her, as if he is seeing her through gauze. He walks right up to her and kisses her briefly on the lips. Her mouth, soft and firm, puckers to kiss him back. He picks up her suitcase and takes her arm to lead her to their train.

In the train, she sits opposite him, trim in her neat blue suit, a rope of pearls swaying as she leans towards the window to watch the countryside rush past, telling him to watch out for her favourite bridge beyond Rochester.

'You know Kent well, Elizabeth?'

'Yes, we had relations near Hythe.'

'You and Alan?'

He mentions Alan's name deliberately. Where is Alan this weekend, he wondered? What has he been told? Late last month, Eva had written Charles a letter, ending their relationship. She was returning to Belfast for the rest of the year and didn't want to see him again. Her main grievance was he couldn't make up his mind about their relationship. 'I don't quite know what you want from me' was how Eva put it. Charles had to agree with her, if he was being honest. He had decided there and then he would ask Elizabeth to come away for a weekend with him. On the advice of a friend in the Embassy who understood the need for discretion, he had phoned a small hotel in Hythe and booked them in for a night. The distance from London was perfect for a short weekend, under an hour to Folkestone and then a taxi up to Hythe.

She ponders his question and then runs her hand down along her skirt. He admires the firm lines of her legs in her tan stockings.

'No. Never with Alan, in fact. I haven't been back in years.'

She looks out the window again, up at the darkening sky and continues, after a few moments pause.

'They were relations of m…m…my…'

She begins to stammer and, unusually, gives up the attempt to finish her words, picking up her book instead.

Another lover, Charles wonders and feels a stab of jealousy. Maybe that Irish writer.

He reaches down for his novel and as he opens it, a letter falls out. It lands at Elizabeth's feet. She scoops it up and without glancing at it, hands it to him.

'A letter from one of your other admirers, no doubt.'

She teases him, smiling to mitigate any sting.

He glances down at it. Eva's last letter. He feels himself blushing under Elizabeth's amused gaze.

'Probably a bill,' he mutters.

'On such pretty paper?'

The envelope is light mauve, to match Eva's elegant writing paper. One of the signs of her trust fund wealth. He curses his own carelessness.

'So, where is Alan this weekend,' he parries, 'off somewhere for work?'

She looks at him quizzically and he is sorry he has asked so bluntly.

'No, at home, I believe. Angela and her chap are calling around for dinner this evening.'

She sits up to face him, brushing down her skirt.

'And, while we are on the subject. I've told Alan I'm visiting Angela's cousin Evelyn Derrick this weekend in Maidstone. Angela knows all about our trip. I prefer not to bother Alan with…well with facts.'

He nods, the look on her face more like the everyday Elizabeth he knows, that dream-like look evaporated. He begins to imagine the conversation with Angela about this weekend, somewhat against his will.

'So, Hythe? Do you know it well?'

'Yes, I lived there as a child.'

That surprises him. He had always assumed that she had lived in Ireland as a child.

'Did you?'

'Ireland until I was seven, then Kent. We spent the summers in North Cork and the rest of the year in Dublin. When we moved here, that was what I really missed most. Summers in Bowen's Court. The fields around Farahy. Dublin, well, not as much.'

'So, I chose well?'

'Very well.'

'You know,' he says, looking at the date on his newspaper. 'It's exactly four months since we met. January twenty-seventh.'

She sighs and says something but a sudden rattle of the train drowns it out.

He looks at her question. She repeats herself, speaking more clearly.

'Four months. How did I bear to wait four months?'

They take a taxi from Folkestone to the hotel, and as they approach Hythe, the marsh swings into view, cutting off a brief glimpse of grey sea, heavy rain clouds on their way from over the Channel. He peers out of the window anxiously.

'I forgot my raincoat. Who expects rain at the end of May?'

'I brought mine. Being Irish, I suppose. Never mind. We can buy you one.'

'But I have one…back in London.'

'Then you will have two. It shan't go to waste.'

He likes her tone of command.

Banks of light pink, wispy shrubs all along the road as they approach the town, perched above them on a steep hill. She draws his attention to the lovely whimsy of the colours as they fly past the window of the taxi, a delight in the dull, overcast light.

'Tamarisks,' she exclaims. 'I had forgotten about them. Look Charles, all in bloom to welcome us.'

He signs the register in the hotel in Hythe. It is more of a small inn than a hotel. The Ram's Head, built into the hill, the rooms and corridors dark and narrow inside. He is watched by a real ram's head, mounted on the wall, its glassy eyes sceptical as he fills out the register. Mr and Mrs Charles Ritchie, Whitehall, London. Elizabeth takes off a glove to touch the petals in the shallow bowl of white roses on the counter, the one with her wedding ring, he notices with approval. The pleasant young woman, wife to the proprietor as she is quick to inform them, pauses in her recital of the restrictions on the hotel menu and is pleased.

'Yes, aren't they a treat! The first from my garden this year, as sweet as you please.'

She takes one and hands it to Elizabeth.

'For you. I'll bring up some more lately.'

Elizabeth smiles her gratitude and pins it on her blouse.

'These must the first roses in England.'

'We always get the earliest flowers here. Kent is the garden of England.'

'Yes. I remember. We always had roses for my birthday in early June.'

'That reminds me,' Charles breaks in, 'I've booked dinner for your birthday. That place off Baker Street. Remember?'

She smiles back conspiratorially. Another plan beyond this weekend. A future assumed.

'You know Hythe?' The young woman asks her.

'A little.'

Elizabeth is still being pleasant but unwilling to continue the conversation. The young woman returns to explaining about butter and asks for their ration books.

He stands patiently, a little bored with the chatter, wondering when she had been there before and with whom. So much of her life unknown to him.

The young woman leads them up the narrow stairs to their room,

'Careful,' she calls, 'there is no light here. Mind your step.'

They stand in the bedroom, and stare at the large bed, covered in a shiny red eiderdown.

'Like a cardinal's cape,' Elizabeth offers, more to break the silence and he laughs, but something about the closeness of the room makes them uneasy and unwilling to stay.

She moves to the window and peers at the narrow strip of grey sky above.

'Oh, damn this rain. I want to show you the town. Let's go and get you a proper coat.'

They find a small gentleman's outfitters. The old man in charge defers to her wifely opinion, as they try a number of coats, most of them too short for his tall frame. Finally they find something they all agree on.

'The fawn, I think, Madam,' the old man looks at Elizabeth, his eyebrow raised, both ignoring Charles as he stands there, feeling foolish in the full-length mirror.

She takes the sleeve and pinches the material lightly, knowingly between her thumb and her forefinger.

'Hmm, yes. On the whole, I agree.'

This must be what it is like to be married, Charles thinks, and the thought is not completely agreeable. She must do this all the time with Alan, picking out shoes and frowning at the length of trousers. Did Alan tell her what to wear? That trim suit she had on. Did he watch her try it in on this morning and tell her which shoes to wear? Charles begins to imagine removing it himself. He hands over his clothing coupons and they leave.

With his new coat on, they brave the light rain and walk down towards the sea. With a light scarf thrown over her head and her coat buttoned up, Elizabeth looks like an experienced country woman or so he tells her. As they walk, she points out the line of Martello towers further along the coastline, set between the marsh and the sea.

'That's Romney Marsh,' she tells him, her hand pressing companionably into his arm as they stroll in the direction of the beach, the air dry, with a strong scent of salt. As they walk, unprompted, she talks about her childhood here.

'When we came here first, you know, I was desperately lonely for home and for my father. He was in hospital and we weren't allowed to see him for nearly a year. To console myself, I pretended Hythe was an island, cut off from the rest of England. At first, I hated England and the English and so that made me happy. Hythe was our island and the sea would never come back.'

She pauses to look back at the town, a slightly quizzical look disturbing her face. He has so many questions but confines himself to one.

'You never said you knew it so well. Was this a good idea?'

'It's perfect. I haven't been back for years, since I was twelve to be precise. I'm glad to be here now. With you.'

He was about to ask her more when she pointed back at the town and made him look upwards.

'Look, the town has crept right uphill, way past the church. When I was a child, the hill was still all fields and now look at all those new houses.'

He looks up at the sky.

'This rain is getting heavier, we should turn back.'

'Nonsense, just a spot of rain.'

Barbed wire keeps them from the beach and as they walk, all the villas are deserted, the windows boarded up. Near the beach, they find a shelter with a wooden seat and watch the dark clouds roll in from the channel. Inside the shelter, she takes off her scarf, pats down her hair and closes her eyes while he smokes.

'Ah, bliss to have no writing today or tomorrow. My eyes ache from it.'

'I must say, I simply can't imagine how you keep writing, with all of this going on.'

He gestures ahead to the dull mass of clouds, in the direction of France.

She opens her eyes to ask.

'All of what?'

'London. The air raids, everything? Death, at any moment.'

She thinks about it briefly.

'Well, some more sleep would be heavenly but, do you know, in a queer way, I think it all helps.'

'In what way?'

'I've always felt a little out of step with the world, ever since I was a child. Now that the rest of the world has come unstuck, it makes me feel less of a lunatic than usual, I suppose. Is that ghastly of me to find something good in this awful cruelty?'

He stares at her in disbelief. Her tone is light but she is clearly in earnest.

'You? Out of step? Elizabeth, you are the most sociable being I know.'

She looks gratefully at him and strokes his sleeve.

'Nice coat. We chose well. Am I? Outside, perhaps. Inside, well, that's another matter. I face into chaos. This constant feeling of being somehow un-located. Cut off. Like Hythe.'

'And yet you write, every day, without fail?'

'Well, it's living in a world I can understand. A world I can make sense of. If that doesn't sound crazy, Charles? '

She looks up at him. Her tone is light but she is in earnest and wants to see his reaction. Angela once told him that when Elizabeth spent her mornings writing, sometimes she had sweat on her brow coming out of her study.

'Not at all.'

'And it also helps me see clearly.'

'And so being in this war, with all that so close,' again he gestures towards the sea, 'it helps you write?'

'Yes, it does. The world is so much more itself that ever before, frightening, more alive, more vulnerable, more exposed. Writing is the only thing that makes sense of it. Somewhere safe to test it all out.'

She pauses, struck by that word.

'Safe. Safety. That's exactly what's missing in the outside world, for us all. It's the same when one is in love. That's usually what we write about, isn't it. Love, and death.'

He risks a question.

'Have you often been in love?'

'Once or twice...?'

He pauses and almost asks, 'At the moment...?' but something stops him, and she draws in a breath and looks directly at him. She watches as he starts and then fails to ask a question. Is she in love now?

He is afraid of knowing the answer to that question. More than that, he is afraid that she will ask him the same question?

Sometime during the night he wakes to the sound of rain falling on a table near the window. He gets up to close the window, careful not to wake her. Her large glass brooch and her pearl beads lie on a table under the window and they feel damp as he touches them, caught in the light drizzle of rain blowing in from the window. He fetches a towel to dry them off and, as he passes the bed, she turns in her sleep, the light sheet falling from her back. He marvels again at the youthfulness and smoothness of her body. What most delighted him was the clean lines, the shapely strength. All through dinner, the awkwardness had grown and at one point, she told him that too much is depending on this night, and they can simply sleep side by side. In answer, he takes her hand and leads her upstairs. He insists on undressing her and she stands in the centre of the room, naked, her eyes slightly closed, and a soft murmur from her as he explores her body with his hands, gently stroking her neck, her arms, her shoulders, and a kiss here and there on her body, slow, unhurried. Standing there, wordless, he sees another woman, not the capable woman he first glimpsed, or the bright intelligent woman he has come to know, but a lover, more beautiful than any other woman he has made love to, silent, gentle, wordlessly rapt in the pleasure of his touch and of his body. He thinks of Eva, her passion, her energy and her desire for him always like a competition or a battle and he regrets the time spent with her and not with Elizabeth. With the window safely shut and soothed by the gentle patter of rain against the glass, he gets back into bed and covers her with the sheet, her face unbearably innocent, smooth and untroubled in the slant of light falling in from the street.

He wakes for a moment, with an awareness of her standing over him in the early morning light. Later in the morning, the sudden clash of church bells nearby wakes him up again, and he finds the bed empty and her clothes gone. Her handbag is perched on the dressing table by the window and her pillow lies next to him, and he moves towards it, catching her perfume as he does so. The room is dim, with a sliver of bright sunlight across the ceiling and he struggles out of the bed, finding his book has fallen on the floor. When he picks it up, he notices that Eva's letter is gone. Had Elizabeth read it? He dresses quickly and then makes his way downstairs. The young woman at reception stops him, and points at a bunch of roses in a vase on the desk before her.

'Oh there you are, Mr Ritchie. I've just cut these for…your wife. Can I trouble you to give them to her?'

He thinks, the receptionist knows that Elizabeth is not his wife, that her wedding ring has nothing to do with him. Such instincts come with running a hotel, he supposes.

She holds out the small posy, tied with a neat red bow.

Hythe 1942

'I'm not sure if she has gone out,' he says, taking them with a smile. 'She may still be at breakfast.'

'Oh, no, she's finished breakfast and asked about morning service. Our church is just down the hill. Service should be finished by now.'

'I'll take them down to her,' he promises. 'Can you prepare our bill? We leave at three, if you could order us a taxi.'

Blinking, he stands in the street outside the hotel and looks around him. The day has cleared up, and the sun is finally out, transforming the narrow lane of the night before into a pretty little street. He walks down the steep lane towards the church, passing people in their Sunday best, feeling self-conscious carrying the roses in his hand. Why did she suddenly decide to go to church? From what he knows of her, he doesn't imagine that she is a fan of Sunday service. The church swings into view, a few people still lingering around the gate and he smiles at the Vicar in the centre of this group. Trust me, his smile assures the Vicar, I am a man who is not going to steal the chalice or the lead off the roof.

He walks up into the church. Empty, with the pleasantly fatty odour of recently quenched candles. He turns and stands in the porch, surveying the graveyard. All at once he sees her, at some distance from the church standing under a tree. He walks over to her as quickly as he can and she starts up slightly at the crunching of the gravel under his shoes. As he approaches, he holds out the bunch of roses to her. To his relief, she smiles and takes them.

'Oh, she is kind, that girl. I told her I was coming here, and look, she went out and picked these for me.'

She takes the roses and kneels to place them on the grave in front of her, like a monarch laying a wreath at a memorial. Charles looks down. It is a corner grave, a little untended, with grass growing all round it, sticking up in uneven tufts. He stands by her side to read the words on the small mossy tombstone. The sun is bright now but in this corner of the graveyard, everything is dimmed by the branches of the lime tree overhead, swaying in the breeze. There is a harp engraved on the small granite headstone and the words below are enveloped in dark moss. He reads:

> *To the memory of Florence Isabella Pomeroy Bowen, Née Colley,*
> *beloved wife of Henry Cole Bowen,*
> *Bowen's Court, County Cork, Ireland.*
> *Born Dublin 1866. Died Hythe 1912.*
> *'Here we have no abiding city, for we wait for the city to come.'*
> *Hebrews 13:14.*

Her mother. He had no idea. Thirty years ago. What would Elizabeth have been then? Early teens at most?

He suppresses an urge to shiver, the distant sound of voices at the gate a welcome reminder of an outer world. This is a pleasant place, for a grave, he tells himself, not at all convinced. Near a shaded corner, some lime trees screening off the town of Hythe, a few birds chirping happily overhead, the swish of grass being scythed somewhere nearby. Why is her mother here and not in County Cork? He watches the firm lines of her shoulders as she kneels to pluck a few weeds, the wind the only noise. Her weeding done, she stands up and reads out the words in front of her.

'Here we have no abiding city, for we wait for the city to come....'
She talks as if to some polite stranger.

'I was so angry with father when I saw that inscription. Poor Father, it wasn't even his idea. One of the aunts insisted on it. They were always too much for him.'

Her voice quieter than he had ever known it, the light chatty tone chilling him. The few remaining parishioners have now left the churchyard and they are alone with the chirping birds and a few stray butterflies and the quiet, frightening grave.

More for himself, he reaches over and takes her hand. She holds on to it with a tight grip.

'Why were you angry?'

She keeps her eyes on the gravestone, her fingers gripping into his knuckles, her tone as if describing some amusing childhood tantrum.

'Oh, the impertinence of it, I suppose. The certainty of this city to come. I was a very opinionated twelve-year old, you know. I wanted to see her again and when I realised that I wouldn't, well, I suppose I never really trusted anything again.'

She stops and he wants to tell her that she was right, that, for example, he himself wasn't to be trusted. But, of course, she knows that.

'No abiding city. That was clear to me, innocent little moon calf that I was. She had kept me close, detained me in childhood. I knew she was sick, father was very clear about that. It never occurred to me that she would die. He should have warned me.'

Having begun to talk, it looks like she won't stop. He keeps quiet, longing to smoke, to move over and kiss her, anything. He wants her to stop and he wants to get away from this civilised, neglected place. But he stays where he is and listens to her.

She stands there, her eyes fixed on the grave and then turns to look at him, her eyes dry and clear, his unexpectedly clouded and teary.

He asks, more out of at a loss for anything else to say.

'Did you often return here?'

She shakes her head.

'No, just that once to see the headstone. Father tried to insist on more visits but I dug in my heels.'

She looked back to the grave, her face calm.

'When you mentioned Hythe, I thought, no. Not a good idea. But then, I decided I could just wander past this churchyard, on my own. No one would see me. I would walk in or I could just keep on walking past. She would understand. She understood everything.'

She pauses, dry-eyed and he watches her closely.

'But, in the end, I found that I could walk in. Nothing lasts. Not even the horror of being here, of seeing her name on the stone, the cruelty of those words.'

She lets his hand go and stoops down again to kiss the gravestone. Then she stands up and takes his hand, her face still dreamlike as he had first seen it on the platform in St Pancras Station.

'Lunch darling, and then the three o'clock train.'

Island House
May 1942

Charles drives them to her house late on a May evening, in an unexpected downpour of summer rain and he is shocked by the gloom that greets them. His heart sinks at the grimness of the old place, stone walls stained by damp, dark windows, the drabness of it all in the pouring rain. This deepens as the unmistakable odour of dank water rises to meet them when Elizabeth pushes open the front door. Soaked in the short run from the car, they stand in the darkened hall in silence, the shuttered windows blocking out the light of the May evening. And then Elizabeth calls out a resounding hello into the vastness of the empty house. At this, Charles hears a door swing open somewhere nearby and a woman moves swiftly towards them out of the darkness, an oil lamp in one hand, the flickering light dancing right up to the roof above them, as in a cavern. She puts down the lamp, wiping her hands on her apron and takes hold of Elizabeth.

'Well now.'

Elizabeth bursts into happy chat, her voice filling the empty hall and echoing up to the ceiling.

'Late and it's all my fault, Teresa. We had drinks in Mitchelstown that went on too long,' Elizabeth tells her, smothered in her embrace.

'I've kept you up. You should be in bed.'

He watches as Teresa immediately begins to fuss around her, feeling her coat and tutting, Elizabeth submitting happily to her clucking and her orders.

'Never mind bed, look at you, soaked with this shocking rain. Get that coat off you. I'll have the kettle on in a second. Tea and a whiskey is what you need.'

Elizabeth laughs with delight and turns to motion him forward. He has kept a fixed smile on his face as the old woman seems determined not to notice him during all her ministrations.

'Teresa, this is Charles Ritchie, our good friend from London. His first time in County Cork in summer and he is thoroughly soaked. I am ashamed of our terrible weather.'

Teresa turns to give him her hand.

'You're very welcome indeed, Mr Ritchie, and I hope you enjoy your time with us. The weather is set to turn, or so they say.'

He feels the warm grasp of her hand, the roughness of her palm a welcome feeling in this dank barracks. He thinks, if the hall is like this, how damp must the beds be? He wonders about sleeping in his new raincoat. Teresa takes a moment or two to peer into his face in the dim light of the lamp, and, apparently satisfied with what she sees, picks up the lamp and hands it to Elizabeth. He can see her more clearly now, an elegant figure in the dark hall with her slim, upright figure and her steel grey hair tightly bound.

The old woman runs her hands lovingly along Elizabeth's arm.

'Now. In with you. There's a fire lit in the Library and in the two bedrooms, and the sheets have been aired in the kitchen. The tea will be wet in a minute.'

'Tea would be the very thing. Charles, take this lamp and go up and get settled in. You are the first door on the right. Teresa and I

Island House May 1942

will get the tea going.'

He hesitates, unwilling to make his way up the uninviting gloom of the stairs. She hands him the lamp.

'Get out of those wet things, this place is plagued with draughts and you will be in a consumption,' Elizabeth tells him, sounding just like the old woman.

The old woman turns and makes her way down in the dark towards the stairs while Elizabeth moves towards the Library, a faint glimmer from the fire evident from the open door. He feels compelled to ask.

'May I help either of you? The stairs may be dark.'

From down the hall, out of the gloom, comes an amused chuckle from Teresa.

'Indeed Mr Ritchie, I could walk the length and breadth of this house blindfolded, and so could herself.'

Early next morning he wakes just after first light, and washes and dresses quickly in the dark room. His bed is large, the sheets reassuringly fresh and the room stuffed with heavy Victorian furniture, yet there is something still unpleasantly overwhelming about the room, the high ceilings, the gilt mirrors over the marble fireplace. Elizabeth insisted he return to his own room late last night after supper, straight across the landing from her own.

'Teresa wouldn't like it,' she whispers as she kisses him for a final time and then pushes him out.

His vast, chilly bedroom is at a corner of the house and he has a bad night's sleep, longing for the warmth of Elizabeth's body next to his, and the reassurance of her steady breathing, sleeping by his side. At one point, somewhere between dreaming and waking, he wakes to see the dim outline of a figure standing by the window.

'Elizabeth,' he called out happily into the dark room, with a sliver of light from the parting in the curtain giving a faint light to the standing figure. Now, in the light of the morning, he knew it was a dream, that no human eye had been watching him as he slept.

Fully awake, he crosses to the window and drags open the heavy brocade curtains. The room is filled suddenly with a dazzling brightness, chasing away the phantoms of the night. He stoops down to open the window. The rain from the previous evening has cleaned the air, and the early morning sun, still slanting low, lights the sparkling blades of grass glittering with moisture outside. He leans out of the window to smell the fresh morning air. Across from the house, leading down the avenue, the hedgerows are in full white flower, as if snow had fallen overnight. He lights a cigarette and smokes at the window for a few minutes, delighting in the freshness on his face, tingling like a mountain stream, while the avenue of lime trees leading to the house shiver slightly in the morning breeze. His first day at Bowen's Court.

He crosses the high-ceilinged corridor to listen at Elizabeth's door. The sounds of a typewriter. He smiles and makes his way downstairs, pausing at the high Venetian window to look out over the plantation of spruce behind the house. Still untouched by the early morning sun, it is a dark mass advancing on the house. At the bottom of the stairs there is a bust on a pedestal. He stops to look. A Bowen ancestor, perhaps? No. Wellington. The Iron Duke. From across the hall a portrait of Oliver Cromwell meets his eye, sceptical, solid. He wonders at the wisdom of displaying such a picture but then again reflects that this is Elizabeth's own country and she presumably knows it best.

The doors of the four downstairs rooms are open and he peers into each room. The Hall, as Elizabeth calls it, where they ate supper, is without a fire but the crackle of sticks burning leads him into the Library. It is a room transformed from the vast candlelit cavern where they drank their whiskey after supper last night. Dazzling light, still touched by the pink tints of dawn, pour in from the low slanting

Island House May 1942

glare of the early morning sun, making the room seem as if it were made of glass, transparent. The lush green of the fields seem almost part of the old room. A tray of coffee is set on a low table in front of the fire and, from high above, on the walls, Elizabeth's ancestors look down at him, serene and indifferent to his early morning intrusion. He is grateful for that indifference.

The sound of a door swinging alerts him to Teresa's presence and he wonders about staying where he is. She is in the empty Dining Room where she is fetching some plates down from a large mahogany dresser. Despite her age, she steps down from the chair with the suppleness of a young girl.

'Good morning,' he smiles at her and she turns to look at him, her face polite.

'Good morning Mr Ritchie. Did you find your coffee?'

'Yes, indeed.'

'She has her tray in the bed and last thing I heard just now was the clacking of that typewriter. We won't see hide nor hair of her until lunch.'

He nods.

'I made myself as quiet as possible.'

'She is always working, day and night. Has herself worn out. I'm taking the car into Mallow in a while, she wants all the Irish newspapers ordered for the next two weeks, if you don't mind. Will you have your breakfast in the Library?'

He smiles at her.

'Rather! Alan told me that it was his favourite place for breakfast and to be sure and ask you for some of the Bowen's Court soda bread with rhubarb jam.'

Teresa looks pleased at his mentioning of Alan.

'It was such a pity Mr Cameron is stuck in London. War work, I suppose. The poor man. You'd think they'd give him a break once in a while and we could rest him up here.'

Teresa takes her plates and goes to leave, pausing to remark.

'Wasn't he in the Great War? You'd think that'd be enough for any government.'

As far as Charles knew, Alan was free to travel over this month but Elizabeth made it clear that they would be alone in Bowen's Court for June. He knew what this looked like. The younger man at liberty during the war, the older man still in harness despite his war record.

'I believe he will be here in August, all going well.'

She claps her hand in genuine pleasure.

'Isn't that the best news yet? Now, in with you to the Library and I'll be in with your soda bread and all.'

After breakfast and, all his letters written and ready for the postman, Charles wanders down the hall. The door is wide open and a small basket of eggs is left sitting on the steps, with a paper bag perched on top. Charles goes onto the porch to smoke, the sound of the clacking typewriter overhead. Deckchairs are laid out on the wide porch and ash trays litter the broad limestone steps. With the advancing morning, he watches as the sun climbs higher across the fields outside and lights up the surrounding ring of trees with a greater inviting clarity. He notices that the car is gone. Teresa off in Mallow.

Unwilling to disturb Elizabeth, he wanders out on to the porch and down the front of the house. Now the stone of the house, warmed by the sun, glistens, looking as if a glittering powder would come away in your hand, the many windows each looking longingly on the prospect ahead, the avenue of lime trees in confident new bud. He rambles around the back of the house drawn towards the walled garden. Nettles choke the lavender bushes, still without their blue flowering, and the fruit trees clinging to the old walls are beginning to bud. Apple trees along the wall are covered in pretty white and pink blossom and a few early roses are already showing colour, a lively red here and there. He admires the limestone of the outhouses, and peers inside the dusty windows to see old tables and chairs stacked up and covered in musty beige canvas, stained with damp. One outhouse seems to have nothing but strings of onions hanging from the roof. Each window is cracked and grimy and some of the doors hang open almost hospitably.

Suddenly, there was the sound of a bell tinkling in the walled garden. He walks over to the open door to find a young boy standing there, holding a large, unwieldy looking black bike, much too big for him. Brown-haired, large sherry-coloured eyes, cheeks flushed from his bike ride, the boy is no more than ten, a little startled by the strange man. Charles smiles reassuringly.

'Is Teresa there? I'm here to get the eggs for my Mam.'

'I'm afraid Teresa has gone into Mallow. May I be of any help?'

The boy looks annoyed.

'Teresa said to call up today. Mam has a crowd coming after the match tonight for sandwiches. She needs eggs.'

Charles smiles.

'Actually, I think I can help you to locate the eggs. Come with me. And there's a paper bag with what looks like bull's-eyes sitting on top of the egg basket.'

The boy looks pleased at the mention of the sweets, obviously his real quarry, but still looks a little suspicious.

'I don't want to disturb Mrs Cameron. She got back last night and Mam said Teresa said she's awful busy with the writing.'

'She is. She's typing away like a fury in her room as we speak. We won't disturb her. Leave the bike there and come with me.'

They walk back to the house, and there standing on the porch, her eyes closed and drinking in the morning sun is Elizabeth, a coffee cup in her hand. The crunch of gravel alerts her and she opens her eyes and beams with pleasure when she sees who it is.

'Arthur! There you are. I was looking out for you.'

The boy runs up the last few steps up and then stands before her, suddenly bashful. Elizabeth smiles over his head to Charles as the boy tells her.

'Mrs Cameron, Mam says to tell you that she expects you in for sherry sometime this week, Sunday would be best. After mass. You have to, she says.'

'Then I will. Tell your mother, Sunday it is. This is Mr Ritchie, Arthur, all the way from Canada. He is visiting us for the next two weeks and he might even have stamps for you.'

The boy looks at him with the first flash of interest, and a slight smile, that draws Charles to him.

'Canada? That's far away, isn't it…?' He pauses.

'I don't have any from there.'

Charles pulls out his wallet and searches.

'You are in luck. Here you go.' He hands him two stamps. The boy murmurs his thanks.

Elizabeth claps her hand.

'That reminds me. Mr Cameron sent you over a whole envelope full. All from the BBC. Run in. I've left them on the low table in the Library by the fire.'

The boy does what he is told and she smiles after him.

'Exploring?'

'Yes, I met Arthur in the garden…Why Arthur?'

'Wellington. A distant cousin of my mother's family. I chose it. I am his godmother, by special dispensation from the Bishop of Cork. His mother runs the nearest pub and is a marvel in business. I wish she would take over the running of this place.'

Island House May 1942

The boy runs back, clutching the opened envelope.

'Can you please say thank you to Mr Cameron?'

'You can thank him yourself, he will be here next month. Now can you manage the eggs on the bike? Teresa has packed them all tightly.'

Arthur looks scornful, as if a few eggs would daunt him, and stands over it. He pokes the paper bag open.

'Bull's-eyes,' he tells them and then pops two bull's-eyes into his mouth.

At lunch, over the roast duck, he tells Elizabeth how well she is looking.

'I don't feel it. I was up at eight. The family book. I've searched high and low but I can't find a single plan of the building of the house. We seem to have every other scrap of paper but no dratted plans. I won't sleep until I find it.'

'I can have a search, if you like.'

'You are an angel. Just have a look through those boxes in the Library on the table. It is driving me to distraction. And how did you find the Blue Room? I thought you might like the morning sun. That side of the house does very well.'

'Not so badly. I woke up to see someone at the window staring at me, at some point. I was hoping it was you.'

She looks puzzled, unsure if he is joking and he realises that he isn't sure himself if he was dreaming, the figure now seems so real. He also recalls clearly, in the light of day, that it was the figure of a man. He tries to keep the tone light as he puts down his fork.

'Does the house have ghosts?'

Teresa has come back into the room with their dessert and answers for Elizabeth, who looks a little perplexed.

'Well, if it has, they stay away from me. I've been here over fifty years and no ghost has ever appeared to me and I've spent long winters alone down in that kitchen.'

Charles ventures a light teasing.

'No ghost would dare, Teresa.'

She smiles and slaps him lightly on the arm.

Elizabeth sits back, and sighs contentedly.

'You know, I have come to the conclusion that the Bowens have taken over the house. All the dead ones, I mean,' she says, pointing up to the portraits. 'And who can blame them? This place was built for large families, not for a solitary pair. In the winter, when we go back to London, they take possession of all of those empty bedrooms upstairs. Every time I come home, I realise that they populate the house now, not me.'

Despite her tone, she is clearly happy and refreshed after her morning's work, sitting at the head of the large table, enjoying her glass of wine. Behind her, one of her ancestors sits in a flowing silk gown with a low cut, her spaniel on her lap, her hair curled and pretty. Next to her a man in eighteenth-century wig and coat, looks grave yet benign, his long narrow face unmistakably like Elizabeth's. Seeing him glance up at the painting behind her, she remarks.

'Pretty, isn't she? That was my Cole ancestress, Jane Cole Bowen. The one who brought all the money. We are all called Cole because of her.'

'I see she brought a spaniel too, as well as all that money.'

She makes a wry face.

'Family legend has it that she died of a bite from the wretched dog. Hydrophobia. At thirty. She can come and haunt me any time but alas she doesn't. Maybe she is in your room. Did you hear yapping?'

'No. It was definitely a man.'

Unwilling to keep talking about it, he looks down at the fork he is holding. A hawk is embossed on the handle.

'Did she bring the hawk as well?'

'No. Cromwell. Did I tell you that story? That hawk earned us all this land. The first Bowen, Colonel Bowen, came over to fight with Cromwell and, for some absurd reason, the Lord Protector took a dislike to one of his hunting hawks and strangled it. In a fit of remorse, Cromwell promised the good Colonel all the land his surviving hawk could fly around and so we got all these lovely fields from Cromwell, thanks to the clever hawk.'

Teresa, bringing in coffee, makes her disapproval plain.

'I don't like talk about that man. That portrait has brought nothing but trouble. Sure the place could have been burnt down because of him.'

'Was the house under threat?'

'Not really. We did have one grievous loss. The IRA camped out here for a weekend and Teresa came over to check on the place, didn't you and frightened them off.'

Teresa chuckles at the memory.

'The place was in a right state, blankets all along the Long Room. I stayed all day but they never came back.'

Elizabeth smiles.

'They were a cultivated lot. One of them borrowed a copy of Kipling's *Kim* from the Library and never returned it. It spoils a set. I always think of him reading Kipling outside the barracks in Mallow when I look along that shelf.'

She stands up and arranges one of the long drapes at the back of the sofa, a luscious-looking pink satin sweeping down from the high ceiling.

'I was admiring that colour. It's like something the Pompadour would have in Versailles,' he tells her.

Teresa chuckles.

'Tell him what the drapes are made from?'

'Corset materials. A bargain in Cork.'

He stares up at the curtains.

The Last Day at Bowen's Court

She laughs. 'I know. Once you are told, it's all you can think of. Corsets. Now, let's go and walk the land and survey the prospect before us.'

Within the first week, with the weather growing warmer and the trees blossoming into full leaf, Charles settles into a routine. The house has charmed him into believing he has always been here. After a solitary breakfast, he works on his letters in the Library until the postman cycles up at ten to deliver the latest batch. Every second day, he arranges for his secretary to phone him at noon, and she keeps him up on all the latest news. After lunch, he and Elizabeth walk the land or take the car and pay visits to Arthur's mother who turns out to be a fashionable young woman who spent ten years in New York and still has something of an accent. Her house is large, the pub well stocked and her taciturn husband stands at the gate to hand Elizabeth out of the car with grave courtesy. At other times, they go to have tea with neighbours in other big houses and always he is quizzed about the war, about Churchill and the Treaty Ports, about the bombing in London. On Sunday, they walk down in the fine sunshine to service in the small church in Farahy and there, afterwards, standing among the Bowen graves, the talk amongst the neighbours is of nothing but the war.

After a few nights in the Blue Room, he suggests moving over to her room, but she demurs, saying that she needs to wake to an empty bedroom, her typewriter waiting for her on her desk with her papers. What Charles doesn't tell her is that his sleep in the Blue Room is never peaceful, the figure by the window never quite returning but somehow a presence lingering, the sense of eyes watching him from the window always keeping him from his rest. Are they Bowen eyes, he wonders, resenting his intrusion?

In the afternoons, when Elizabeth returns to her writing, her family book engrosses her and Charles works in the Library, searching for documents in old boxes, helping her locate letters from the long,

Island House May 1942

tangled history of Bowen's Court. Arthur sometimes calls over to help him and they lift down old boxes, and carefully examine the contents, the boy full of questions about the war and Canada. Charles grows to love this room, the bare wooden floors of the hall heated by the blaze of sunshine, the scent of polish and of the old beams of wood filling the Library with a warm, spicy scent, the green smell of summer foliage from the fields outside. The brilliant yellow of the furze bush by the stables sometimes fills the lower rooms with the faint scent of coconut.

Some days, with Teresa working out in the walled garden and Elizabeth immured in her room, he wanders the house alone. Charles walks in and out of bedrooms, with windows all flung open to dispel the dankness of rooms shut up and unused all winter. He feels no sense of the surveillance that disturbs his nights. One sultry afternoon, he goes up to his bedroom to lie down and smoke and test the atmosphere. The peace of the room and the sound of distant mowing and the stray butterflies fluttering into the room make him drowsy. He wakes to find Elizabeth lying beside him, asleep also, fully dressed, one hand resting gently on his arm, her face peaceful and like that of a girl, a pillow grasped within her arms for comfort. He falls asleep again and wakes to Elizabeth's light oath.

'Damn.'

'What is it?'

'Teresa. She just popped her head around the door.'

He sits up and then turns to take her in his arms. 'Just as well,' he says and kisses her.

One morning, on the phone, his secretary mentions that Eva is back from Belfast, called in that morning to see him and insisted on getting his address.

'I'm sorry, Mr Ritchie, but she was very firm about it. I felt that I had to tell her.'

He reassures his secretary but curses Eva and her persistence. The next day, he comes back from Mallow to find a parcel on the hall table with his name on it, and Eva's clearly marked as sender. He asks Teresa when it arrived and she tells him the postman came over especially in the morning to deliver it. Damn, he thinks, Elizabeth has seen it. However, nothing is mentioned at dinner and he takes Eva's parcel and leaves it unopened on his bedside table.

Walking back home on the lower avenue one evening, he encounters Teresa on a bicycle, and she gets off to walk with him courteously back up to the house.

'Are you enjoying your visit here?'

She asks him, anxious to know that he is happy here.

He nods his head vigorously,

'It's like living on an island in this house. Every time I come back, I feel I should have a boat to ferry me up here.'

They pause to watch the flight of birds over the field, a full moon glowing with a golden light just above the church steeple. Charles thinks, only in Ireland in late May can such summer evenings seem unending in their gentleness, as if no real darkness can ever descend on such a landscape of gentle unending light.

'You must know the house better than anyone else?'

'Indeed and I do. I remember her mother, God be good to her, being driven through those gates back down by the church. Torchlight the whole way up. The young bride, in her red cloak, so pretty. The men took the horses away and pulled the carriage up to the door of the house, just to welcome her, and she crying with happiness.'

She pauses as they approach the house.

'It's a shame she wasn't brought home to rest in the church below. I don't know where they buried her in England.'

Hythe. He wants to tell her, a pretty little churchyard in the town, as lonely as you can imagine. But he knows he shouldn't tell her.

'And then the master himself. Her father. All that worry and work. I remember walking with him on this very path, and his voice cracked with all the endless talk and I said, Master Henry, let's walk along now and just look at the trees and no more talk. And it did the trick. Sure, we were the same age. Played together as children. If I couldn't say it, who could?'

In the evenings, they listen to the latest news from the BBC in the Library, with Teresa joining them. Charles tries not to comment too much on the bad news from France and from Russia, as bad as it could be. He knows he will have to get back to London soon, but these precious two weeks are the first leave he has taken since the war began and he intends to stay.

The good weather holds and each dusk seems eternal to Charles in these enchanted fields. After dinner, they sit on cushions on the front steps, the radio playing dance music deep in the house, their glasses scraping against the stone of the steps. They talk until the sun finally slips behind the fir trees. They watch the rooks crossing the sky before them in what seem like flocks of thousands, their cries filling the silence, hordes of them settling like a plague on one tree or another then, all of a sudden, flying upwards in swirling circles.

That night, he awakens again to a stronger sense than ever that he is being watched. Nobody is there but unseen eyes from the window keep him awake until dawn.

The following morning, a letter comes and Elizabeth tells him she must go to Dublin for a few days and asks if he will come with her. She is writing reports for the Ministry of Information and needs his advice, she wants access to De Valera but it is proving impossible. He is curious to see Dublin but the thought of leaving this house makes him unexpectedly sad.

'You know how these diplomatic circles work, you can help me. Do come with me, I can show you Dublin. We can stay in the Shelbourne. Such glorious cream teas.'

'I daren't mention cream teas in London. They would never forgive me.'

On this, their last night, Arthur cycles over to collect Canadian stamps that Charles has kept for him and Teresa promises the boy supper and tells him she will make up a mattress for him in her room. His mother has a wake to go to and doesn't want him cycling home to an empty house. Arthur is delighted at the chance to stay and after dinner sits at Elizabeth's feet.

'Tell us a ghost story, Mrs Cameron,' he pleads.

'But you will have nightmares, Arthur, and I will be in big trouble with your mother and you know what that's like.'

She teases him but he persists and she relents, the evening staying warm as the colour fades from the sky.

Teresa sits with her newspaper, a large pot of tea before her, just out of the rays of the still warm sun, Arthur at her feet with the last of the bull's-eyes, sprawled on a rug, looking up at Elizabeth who has her coffee and brandy by her side. Charles smokes, his whiskey at his feet, the clink of ice as he lifts it up, the white of the whitethorns like lace before them in the glowing dusk light.

'Many years ago, my wicked ancestor, Colonel Bowen came to Ireland with even wickeder Oliver Cromwell to fight and to plunder.'

Arthur smiles, liking the sound of all that plunder. She pauses to light her cigarette.

'Meanwhile, back on his estates in Wales, his unfortunate wife was at peace, glad to have her husband away from her. You see, she was a pious woman and her husband had shocked her very much by offering five hundred pounds to any man who could tell him the truth about God's existence.'

Teresa snorts.

'I'd tell him. Give me the five hundred pounds. God is in his Heavens and watching you very closely, my bucko. That's the whole story. Now, hand over my money.'

Arthur frowns up at her for disturbing the story and she makes a face of mock apology and puts her finger to her lips, promising to stay quiet.

'Then one night, Mrs Bowen went to her bedchamber with her maids to pray and to retire for the evening when, all of a sudden, a high wind blew up outside and all the windows began to rattle.'

Arthur sits up, frightened despite himself, but hanging on her every word.

'The bed began to shake and the curtains around the bed flap and the candles blew out. The terrified women threw themselves on their knees and prayed with all their might for this ungodly tempest to stop.'

Teresa watches her with open amusement, glancing down from time to time at the enraptured face of the boy. Charles listens to her voice, Elizabeth's, on this terrace, with the cry of the returning rooks in the distance and the faint roar of a motorbike on the Mallow road. It is the voice of a much younger woman, of a girl really, just as young as her beautiful body and he knew that he could listen to it forever.

'Their prayers were in vain because a figure appeared before them in the darkened chamber, the dark outline of a man, watching them from the window as they lay terrified on the bed. Clutching their prayer books, they cried out to God to banish this apparition. Holding her bible, our brave Mrs Bowen stood up to order the apparition away. It was then that she recognised the figure looming before her. It was her husband, Colonel Bowen, who had gone to Ireland, with Cromwell.'

The figure in his bedroom, Charles suddenly wonders. Alan?

'I knew it,' the boy exclaims. 'He got killed in Ireland. That very night.'

The Last Day at Bowen's Court

Elizabeth draws on her cigarette and pauses.

'Well, you might think that, Arthur, and so Mrs Bowen thought and they fetched a clergyman into the house the very next day to pray for the dead soldier. Letters were sent out to Ireland asking for news and telling of the apparition…But…'

She pauses for dramatic effect.

'Soon they learnt that Colonel Bowen was…still alive and well and harrying the Irish and conquering all this land around here. They all prayed with thanks for his continued good luck, although how sincere Mrs Bowen was in her prayers I cannot say and they went about their business and tried to forget about it. To her horror, the very same thing happened again the next night. The windows shook and the bed rattled and something struck at the frightened woman. This living apparition came back to terrorise his unfortunate wife, who prayed to God to deliver her from this persecution for the next wearisome month and no bible could vanquish it.'

The boy sits up. His eyes are large and round and he ponders on the strangeness of the story.

'But how could a living person be a ghost, Mrs Cameron?'

'That's the mystery Arthur, nobody could explain it. That's what makes it even uncanny.'

Teresa stands up.

'Well, we'll never solve it now. It's time for bed, young man,' she said firmly, taking him by the hand.

'Say goodnight to Mrs Cameron and Mr Ritchie and thank them for all the treats today.'

He does so reluctantly, and is led away, the two disappear into the darkening house.

As soon as the footsteps die away, Charles takes Elizabeth's hand and strokes it.

Island House May 1942

'I'll miss all of this in London. I've come to love your island house.' She squeezes his hand.

'It's your home now. Your home in Ireland.'

He can hear steps coming back down the hall and goes to disengage his hand from hers but, to his surprise, she keeps a firm hold of it as Teresa comes back out on the porch.

'What time for the breakfast?' she asks, her tone calm, her eyes firmly avoiding the hands being held below her. He wonders at Elizabeth's sudden possession of his hand. Then it strikes him. Eva.

'Seven, I think. That should give us enough time. The plan is to catch the Dublin train in Mallow at ten. That should get us up into Dublin for lunchtime.'

Teresa nods, her face set into blankness and turns to go, the boy calling her from the kitchen. They stay sitting there on the porch, the sun slipping down behind the lime trees, the rooks making the final journey across the demesne, their black mass now dark and indistinguishable from the approaching darkness of evening, the only sounds their cries.

'I think I'll visit you in the Blue Room tonight, if you like. I don't like the thought of any other Bowen sharing you, even a dead one.'

He nods and smiles and reaches for his whiskey, the rattle of ice echoing outwards to disturb the rooks in their blackened tree tops.

At the Shelbourne 1942

Elizabeth slips out of bed to watch him sleep, and taking a sheet of paper, begins a letter to him. 'My Darling, My Darling, My Darling.'

She pauses, and holds the pen aloft. The hotel room is warm, the strong sunlight creeping along the heavy velvet curtains. Charles lies there, free of the sheets, clasping a pillow within his thin, strong arms, sleeping with a kind of concentrated intensity, his face vulnerable and soft without his dark-rimmed glasses. It is just past seven o'clock and already she can hear a trolley wheeled along the corridor outside, making floorboards creak. She is afraid that he will wake up, ending this precious moment of contemplation but Charles sleeps on with complete absorption.

She continues to write, 'To turn from everything to one face is to find oneself face to face with everything.'

With a sheet wrapped loosely around her, she sits in a deep comfortable armchair at the end of the double bed and continues her love letter to him, a letter she can never show him.

'For me, it as if we have walked a new country together. Each place has becomes ours alone and never simply mine again. Farahy,

Regent's Park, Hythe, here in Dublin. I sit looking at your beloved face, and the truth is that, in the short months since we met, yours is the only face I really see. I know now that will never change for me.'

She stops. A light knock at the door. She pushes the letter under the chair and creeps over to fetch in the morning tray. Charles stirs and murmurs but burrows under a pillow determined to sleep. With her coffee beside her, she takes up her letter.

'Death has surrounded us from the start, but somehow, because of this, the accidental miracle of our first meeting is made even more precious. I have never felt more alive than when I am with you or thinking about you. From the first moment, I saw a glimpse of something, a promise of an elsewhere, and now it is fulfilled. A question now answered.'

He stirs and she stops writing. The hotel room is on a corner of St Stephen's Green, and the bright sunshine has now filled the room with insistent summer light. The room smells of his body and her perfume from last night, the empty glass of whiskey a fruity tang in the heavy air, her coffee rich and luxurious in the airless room. His long, slender body, tangled in one stubborn sheet, moves as he murmurs and she follows the clean lines, the long legs, the surprisingly powerful thighs, the elegant chest and shoulders, the dark hair at the nape of his neck, fine dark hair thinning at the crown of his head. He is dreadfully self-conscious about it, she knows, but for her, it is a precious part of him, like his dark eyebrows arching his brown eyes. His beloved neck that she kissed not three hours ago. Not know where his mouth began and her mouth ended. The thought of the day, of the phone calls she must make, the letters to be posted, the article to be finished, drives her back to her letter. This letter is for her and her alone, all the things she cannot tell him.

The Last Day at Bowen's Court

'When I wait for you, in the evenings, just before dinner, in those final moments, I feel alive as never before. When we walk and talk, my world expands, transformed into a place of enchantment. The truth is that, in a few short weeks, you have become my inner world. All the rest of my everyday life is something only to be endured until I see your face again. For me, this is only the beginning, the opening moments of a journey together, whatever that turns out to be and the miracle is that somehow we remain alive in this time of death.'

She is startled to see that he has woken up, and is smiling at her.

'Why the frenzy?'

She stops herself from covering up the letter.

'Just some tedious business.'

'The Ministry?'

'More of a love letter, actually.'

She risks a joke as he seems less and less interested.

He sits up and yawns.

'To Churchill, I suppose.'

She nods, wondering if he will insist on reading the letter.

'Yes I confess I do admire him dreadfully. David Cecil told me that Winston read my last report himself or had some of it read to him, at any rate, and said it was a pleasure to have something so lucid on Ireland for once. I was giddy, like an infatuated schoolgirl. Still I didn't change his mind about De Valera, I'm afraid, despite all my pleading for the Irish.'

He yawns again and pushes away the sheet.

'Forget about De Valera. Come back to bed.'

Later that day, she stands on the bridge in St Stephen's Green, waiting for Charles, watching the sky darken. The promise of sunshine in the early morning has vanished and she wonders if she should take

At the Shelbourne 1942

shelter. Charles is late. She has stayed in the Shelbourne all morning, phoning Mr De Valera's office to plead for an appointment, to no avail. A trip by taxi to the British Representative's office has proved fruitless and she phones Alan for advice in London. Alan tells her that he will see a chap he knows in the Dominions Office who works for Eden and will call her back in the afternoon. She thought of telling Alan about her unease, the lurking dread around each corner of the Dublin streets, but he would only insist on calling in one of her aunts and making her go and stay with them.

Something began to unsettle her during her solitary lunch in a noisy café off Grafton Street, a feeling of unease, as if she was somehow draining away. Her stroll through Trinity College under a darkening sky, only served to unravel her further. All the peace of that week with Charles in Bowen's Court has fled her and now she paces around the bridge as she waits for Charles to come. Young matrons with prams walk past, covertly admiring the elegance of her light summer suit, and a surprising number of priests seem to be at leisure to walk around the Green in pairs, whispering comfortably like lovebirds and nodding to the pious who raise their hats as they pass. All during the morning, as she posted letters, phoned sundry relatives and attended her bank manager, something about the remorselessness of the Dublin streets has oppressed her until she longs for Charles and wishes herself back in that hotel bedroom. His name forms wordlessly as a bid for reassurance, an unspoken whisper on her lips as she becomes unstuck in the cheery, bustling streets.

Over the lush trees of St Stephen's Green, silken and fresh in their early summer glory, the blanket of light grey cloud has quenched the sun, threatening rain. Even now, she feels a warning sprinkle and spinning around, she suddenly catches sight of Charles striding towards her, unhurried, confident and she strains to watch him in his blue coat. She takes a grip of the stone balustrade and looks as he moves between the bright colours of the flowerbeds towards the bridge. All sense of being fragmented leaves her as she says it out loud to herself. 'Here is my lover.'

He smiles as he gets nearer and begins talking just in earshot.

'Sorry, Elizabeth, the chap I know in the Embassy says no can do on De Valera. He is more tightly guarded by his retinue than Churchill.'

She shakes her head and takes a grip of his arm.

'Never mind. I have enough for the next report. What a bother about nothing. I'm on his side, why are they so suspicious of me? Oh well, the whiff of the Big House, I suppose. Not to be trusted in this New Ireland. Time for tea, I think. We have earned it.'

They move off towards the hotel, her arm lightly caught in his.

'Well, at least I've bagged the Archbishop for tea tomorrow, or as good as.'

He whistles.

'How did you pull that off?'

'Oh, I spun his chaplain some nonsense about a broadcast on Dublin in the Emergency for the BBC. That seems to have done the trick. He will phone back this evening.'

He looks at her admiringly.

'You can talk your way in anywhere.'

'By the by, what exactly does one call an Archbishop? I was trying to recall from Trollope but no one in Barchester was ever anything more than a Bishop.'

'Your Grace. Like a Duke.'

They walk back towards the hotel, her delight in the solid ground of his face animating her. Her world is back in tilt, Dublin now solid ground because he is there. The rain suddenly gets heavier, the lush

At the Shelbourne 1942

vegetation of St Stephen's Green like a mild tropical wilderness, the rain warm and caressing, the scents of the newly watered undergrowth spiced and intimate. They run, laughing, to the entrance and make it there just as a cloudburst scatters the summer crowd in all directions. At the front of the hotel, the bronze nymphs hold up the torches. *Flambeaux,* as her Aunt Myra taught her to call them. This reminds her of something and she stops in the hotel lobby to tell him.

'The things one remembers all of a sudden. Aunt Myra brought me to tea here most Sundays when I was a child. Once she happened to mention that Lady Blessington, a lady novelist of the last century, dropped a very precious locket on the ground right outside the Shelbourne. Her ladyship couldn't find it and spent the rest of her life lamenting it.'

They stand happily under the awnings, watching the sheets of warm rain whip against the luxurious green of the trees opposite. The lobby fills with those caught in the rain, laughing and shaking out their light summer coats as they gain the safety of the hotel.

'I became obsessed with that locket and every Sunday I wandered around the pavements, peering down to find it. I even poked around the gutters with my umbrella until my governess complained. Aunt Myra was so annoyed with me and told me not to be such a goose.'

'What was so precious about the locket?'

'Apparently it had a lock of Lord Byron's hair in it. Lady Blessington met him in Italy in her youth and it was her prize possession. I worshiped Byron as a girl, you see. He was my first passion.' Charles nods, 'I was crazy about Byron when I was a child, too. I used to wander around the woods behind our house, declaiming, "But there is that within me which shall tire Torture and Time and breathe when I expire." Much to my mother's dismay. She was afraid Byron was turning me into a pansy. Now she worries I am a lady killer.'

Not quite liking the turn this conversation has taken, she walks over to the desk to collect her post and the concierge hands her a telephone message. This reminds her of something and she stops in the hotel lobby to tell him.

'Oh dear. I have conjured her up.'

Elizabeth turns to face him, looking a little uncomfortable.

'What do you mean?'

'Aunt Myra. She phoned at lunchtime. She has tracked me down. I swore Teresa to secrecy but the aunts seem to have some sort of collective mind when it comes to my whereabouts.'

He smiles.

'It's no laughing matter. Aunt Myra is proposing herself for tea later today. Do you want to skip off or could you bear meeting her?'

Elizabeth asks the question lightly but wonders if he will hesitate.

After a moment, he replies.

'I'd be charmed. Teresa told me all about her, I'm sure she won't bite me. All part of our training, too, formidable aunts, you know. We are given special instruction in that field.'

'She is the toughest of a pretty tough collection of aunts, I should warn you.'

At this moment, Charles frowns at her and makes an imperceptible nod over her shoulder. She turns, and to her horror, sees Aunt Myra sitting there. Her aunt is on the sofa opposite them in the lobby, her eyes closed apparently asleep, but within earshot. Elizabeth curses inaudibly, not quite believing in this doze.

'Was she sitting there all along?'

She whispers to Charles.

'Yes, watching us. Her eyes just closed the minute I noticed her. Who is it?'

Elizabeth makes a face.

Charles looks at her in mock horror and whispers, 'Not Aunt Myra?'

Elizabeth nods and then takes a deep breath and crosses the lobby to bend down and kiss her aunt awake.

'Bitha!'

Her aunt shakes herself and gives a convincing impersonation of someone roused from slumber. As she recalls, Elizabeth said nothing she wished her aunt not to hear. Calling her tough would be only what she was due. Myra looks around her and grimaces.

'I came in to shelter from the rain and nodded off. How annoying. They must think I've turned senile here.'

'They would never dare to think that, Aunt,' Elizabeth tells her, stroking her arm.

Elizabeth looks down at her aunt's shoes. Dry. Myra has been lying in wait for her. Neatly dressed as ever, trim figure, her iron grey curled hair in perfect order, Myra looks as she always had during Elizabeth's childhood, the picture of confident sociability and someone to keep a sharp eye on. Like writers, Myra is someone on whom nothing is wasted. As she chatters away, everything is noticed and filed away for future reference.

'Aunt. I was just talking about you to Charles and you appear. I was telling him about the Byron locket.'

Myra struggles up to embrace her and to turn graciously to Charles who bows. Myra seems to be about to shake his hand but changes her mind and turns back towards Elizabeth.

'Your memory, Bitha, never fails to frighten me. That awful Byron locket indeed. I told you that story to amuse you and I came to regret it. For months you were trawling the gutters of Kildare Street looking for it, ruining your shoes and my good umbrella. Frau Hoftner was very angry with me.'

Her aunt begins collecting her parcels, as spry as ever, and shakes off

Elizabeth's helping hand. It crosses Elizabeth's mind that her aunt is annoyed with her and she sighs. She is pleased to see her but wonders how long she will impose herself into this precious time with Charles.

'Aunt Myra, this is our friend Charles Ritchie, from the Canadian Embassy.'

Charles, impeccable as ever, takes her aunt's hand and Elizabeth can see, as all women do, the older woman turn a smile of pleasure to this tall, elegant young man smiling gently down at her.

'Mrs Fisher, my pleasure. I hope we are in time for tea, I've been at the Dublin office and tea is what I need.'

He has even remembered her name. Clever man, leading her into the drawing room catching the eye of the head waiter, taking her large bag and parcel into his custody while Elizabeth trails after them like an awkward teenager being brought out from school for high tea.

Her aunt takes the centre seat in the middle of the room and invites Charles to sit by her, relegating Elizabeth to a smaller chair without an armrest. Although over seventy, Aunt Myra looks in full bloom, her hair newly crimped, and her linen suit fresh, a yellow rose pinned to her lapel. The sun has come out again, the trees outside gleam in the wash of the summer rain and, like a floodlight, the beams of early evening light fill the drawing room, glaring around Myra's head like a beacon.

Once ensconced, her aunt is soon in full flow, giving Charles the history of the hotel and its moments of drama, while the waiter hovers with the tea tray and her aunt casts a shrewd glance over the sandwiches, the slightly dry-looking fruitcake.

'Bitha, hand me that parcel nearest to your feet.'

Her aunt delves down deep and produces a cake tin. Without a moment's pause she opens it and takes out a small cream cake and places it on the table, pushing aside the hotel's fruitcake.

'Aunt,' Elizabeth murmurs in mock horror, admiring her audacity.

A passing waitress forgets her training for a moment to stare at this effrontery but her aunt calls her over.

'My dear, can you fetch a cake plate for this as soon as you can?' and the girl scurries off, her training ensuring that she keeps her face blank.

Myra attends to the cake with the full glare of June sunshine, and the shine from the pools of rain outside. Charles bends forward attentively to hand around the cake and Elizabeth herself sits like a penitent maiden on her lowly stool.

'Now, much better for us. Freshly made this morning and you know what a lovely sponge our Aggie makes. She has been my mainstay for years, Mr Ritchie, came with me from home when I married. She sends her love to you, Bitha and wants to know when Alan is coming over to see us, she wants to make him one of his favourite porter cakes.'

All the time, Aunt Myra is glancing at Charles when he is not watching, taking in the well-cut suit, the elegant frame, the polite demeanour.

'August. Aunt, he must work until then. I wrote and told you.'

'And you, Mr Ritchie, how long can you spare in Dublin? You must come and see my garden, all the roses are just out.'

'I must return to London as soon as possible, I'm afraid, my time away is nearly up but I intend to come back to Ireland and would love to see your roses. Regent's Park is glorious at the moment, despite all the grit and glass in the air.'

Aunt Myra shudders.

'London. One hears such horror stories that I simply try and put them out of my mind, with Bitha and Alan right in the centre of it all, and my other niece Angela as well.'

As far as she knew, Charles has another week's leave and this talk about returning to London is new. She feels the solid ground underneath her shift unpleasantly. Just then, somewhat to her relief, a porter comes up and murmurs discreetly that there is a call for her at the main desk.

'Can you take a call from your husband, Mrs Cameron? The operator in London said five minutes.'

She stands up.

'Aunt, that's Alan, he's trying to arrange for me to meet Mr De Valera. This could be my lucky break. Charles, can you protect my aged aunt while I'm away and try and get her to stay awake?'

Aunt Myra slaps her playfully and tells her to give Alan her love. Elizabeth throws Charles an apologetic look, but like most people, he is trapped in the full beam of Aunt Myra's charm, unable and unwilling to move.

She sits into the small dark booth, like a confessional, and waits for the call from Alan and thinks about her Aunt Myra. Always there in her childhood, solid and keeping one on one's toes and that solidity became suddenly precious after her mother's death. Once, when Elizabeth was around fourteen and spending the summer in Dublin with Aunt Myra, her cousin Angela trapped her casually in a bedroom one afternoon and began interrogating Elizabeth about her mother's death. Helpless to stop her, Elizabeth found herself under interrogation, her cousin remorseless as children always are.

'But Bitha, what exactly happened to poor Aunt Florence. What did she die of? Nobody will tell me?'

Crossing the landing with some flowers, Myra had overheard it and sent the girl cousin away with a flea in her ear.

'Angela, you have no business prying. Now, go downstairs and tell your uncle that you are not allowed go out to see the new puppies this afternoon. You can sit in the Library and think about what you have done.'

They watched as the tearful girl cousin, her mouth trembling, made her way out of the bedroom.

'You must forgive her, Bitha, Angela is a year younger than you and still a child.'

Then Myra had taken her in her arms, a rare act for her.

'Bitha, dear, Florence is in all of our hearts, there is no need to speak about her. Florence knows how much we loved her.'

Elizabeth glanced up to see her aunt, her practical aunt, her eyes filled with tears and realised that someone else was missing her mother. For that, Elizabeth always trusted her aunt, even today when she is being punished.

The phone rings, making her jump.

Alan's voice, a little hollow, comes down the line.

'Elizabeth. You there?'

'Yes, Darling. So any luck?'

'Something. Davie has made you an appointment with James Dillon on Thursday. Got a pen?'

She writes down all he has to tell her and there is an awkward silence. He must be wondering why she has left Cork.

'I'm with Myra, dear. She hunted me down and insists on tea. Shall I give her your love?'

Elizabeth is relieved not to have to explain Charles' presence, Myra apparently her only reason for being in the Shelbourne.

'Do. Tell her I'll see her in August. Must dash. Love to all there.'

Before she can say anything else, Alan is gone. Punishment from another quarter. Myra may have told him that she was staying with Charles at the Shelbourne. Or Teresa. More likely Teresa.

When she gets back, Aunt Myra is in full flight on one of her favourite stories and by now Charles looks thoroughly bored, although hiding it manfully.

'So, on the Monday, my friend Henrietta was coming back from the races, you know, for the Bank Holiday, and the rebels had taken over St Stephen's Green, though I suppose I shouldn't call them rebels, should I, after all they run the country now. Anyway, Henrietta made her way up the steps and here into the Drawing Room where afternoon tea had just begun, despite the troops out on the Green and the Countess in full uniform striding around. Henrietta ordered tea but the head waiter had suggested they all go back into the Library instead, as a gun fight was expected. But they all insisted on staying where they were. The most they would do was close the heavy wooden shutters.'

Charles had begun to look around but Aunt Myra touches his elbow and he smiles attentively.

'So Henrietta was just beginning her tea when a bullet came right in through the window, whizzing over her head and shattering the mirror behind her. On the floor beside her, in the heap of glass, was the bullet and a single silk rose, sliced off by the bullet off from the top of her hat. I saw the hat myself. Well, with that, they decided it was time to move back into the Library!'

Elizabeth is aware that a young man is trying to catch Charles' attention and nudges his arm. He jumps up and beckons the young man over.

'Larry, there you are! Mrs Cameron, Mrs Fisher. May I introduce you to my friend?'

A fresh-faced young man stands there politely.

'This is Larry, sorry, Mr Lawrence Scott, my counterpart here in Dublin and an old friend from Oxford.'

The young man bows politely to Aunt Myra and turning to Elizabeth, smiles.

'Do forgive me, but I am a great admirer of your writing, if I may say. Always have been.'

At the Shelbourne 1942

Elizabeth smiles graciously but notes Charles is gathering his things to leave.

'Thank you, Mr Scott. That is very kind of you. Won't you join us for some tea?'

He looks as if he would like to but Charles shakes his head.

'Larry may have a useful lead to the Prime Minister. He's asked me to his club, to meet some chaps there. He knows a writer who knows Mr De Valera, a Cork man, of all things.'

'Really it's extraordinary what sort of people write books,' Aunt Myra chimes in…catching Elizabeth's sardonic look, hastened to add, 'Not you, dear. You always dress so beautifully.'

Charles turns and bows to Aunt Myra,

'Mrs Fisher, it was a pleasure to meet you, please do thank Agnes for the delicious cake.'

'You won't get cake like that in London, or so my friends there tell me, Mr Ritchie.'

With the party breaking up, Aunt Myra also senses it is time to leave.

'Bitha, darling, help me with all of this,' thrusting her bag at Elizabeth. Under cover of all of the activity, the two young men shake hands and depart.

'My shoes are soaking wet. Bring me up to your room, my dear. I need to borrow a pair of your stockings. Angela is calling in for me at six and I can't face the drive out to Killiney in this wet pair.'

Elizabeth thinks of the hotel bedroom as she left it this morning, all the evidence of her night with Charles and then, shrugging, escorts her aunt upstairs.

The room has been tidied and the windows left opened but Charles' dinner jacket hangs over a chair. Aunt Myra looks everywhere but there.

'I haven't been inside one of these bedrooms since your Cousin Lois's wedding and that must be, what, ten years or so? This is a nice room, I must say and a clear view of the Dublin Mountains.'

Her aunt chatters on and on, her sharp eyes take in all the evidence of the room, and Elizabeth longs for her to leave but listens dutifully.

Later that evening, after her aunt has left, she lies down to sleep. The phone wakes her up. It is Charles.

'Elizabeth.'

It sounds noisy wherever he is.

'Are you there? Larry is on to something, but wants me to dine with a few of the legation chaps. Do you mind awfully?'

'Not at all. I have a letter to finish and my drink here. See you later. Don't bother about dining here.'

She puts down the phone and crosses the room to sit on the winged armchair. Something crackles behind the cushion. Her letter to Charles. She fishes it out and begins to re-read. Then picking up a pen she continues to the end. 'You have come to mean more to me than anyone else in my life, Angela, John and Diana, Aunt Myra, Teresa, Alan.' She pauses and then crosses out Alan's name, 'When I am with you, it is as when I write. These are the moments of true living for me and my writing is filled with the sense of being alive that you bring me. My new book is our book, and I write every word for you. In your face are all my dreams realised. When you are an old man, at the end of your life, I want you to remember these words.'

She finishes, signs her name and stands up. The curtains are open and she stands in the open window, the letter in her hand. Over the trees in St Stephen's Green, a faint light can be seen outlining the Dublin Mountains. Through the window, a warm breeze rustles the pages in her hands. Across the street, she can hear waterfowl splashing in the lake. Below her, a car pulls up and the sound of female laughter echoes up to her. She tries not to think of those two young men, polished, charming, in some club nearby as she takes her precious letter and begins to tear it up. She leans forward and releases the fragments of notepaper into the night air, thrusting them away from her. She watches the shower of paper, caught up in a sudden fall of rain, like the climbing roses in the walled garden, the white petals showering the grass at home in Bowen's Court all through June. The fragments of paper flutter in the breeze for a moment and then, shot down rapidly by the sudden downpour, are swiftly dispatched into the muddy ground below. With a slight shiver, she turns and gets into bed, to wait for Charles' return.

Mistakes
London
1942

Elizabeth realises that she has begun to make mistakes. Only the kind of mistakes made by someone in love who fears loss. During a walk around Regent's Park, she makes her first mistake when she finds herself telling Charles what he has come to mean to her. It is, she told him, as if she was talking about someone else, an utter experience of love for her, something that she has never felt before. Some of the phrases from the letter she had written him, written and then torn up, come back to her as she speaks and watches his face as he listens for clues.

It is her first week back from Ireland, the first time in a month they have met since their time in Dublin and that month apart has made her nervous. He phones her to arrange to meet in the park and she suggests he come back with her to the flat, where Alan has organised a sherry party to welcome Elizabeth home. In the Rose Garden, the August scents overpowering in the languid air, his tall figure by her side, the face she has been imaging now finally before her, she suddenly finds the words.

'Charles, can we stop for one minute? Please.'

Mistakes London 1942

They pause to stand, causing a momentary standstill in the wandering happy Sunday crowds and so she takes him to one side, just off the path and looks up into his face, anxious, troubled, while he smiles at her.

'You must know.'

'What must I know?' He looks at her with good-natured concern, his eyes intent on her, tender, a little anxious.

'That you. Us. This time together. I've never felt like this before. You are heady wine, my darling.'

They stand there for a while as she talks and he listens. Those passing by wondered a little at the intensity of this couple standing on the grass. She keeps talking while he watches her.

'I am so grateful for the chance that brought us together.'

He stands, watching her closely, his dark eyes serious and beautiful.

'As am I,' he agrees, waiting for her to continue.

She risks the phrase in her letter, long lost in the gutters of St Stephen's Green.

'All my dreams are in your face.'

She reaches up and runs a finger along his cheek. He takes it and kisses it. For a while, he says nothing and then he does, choosing his words carefully.

'Elizabeth. For me, whatever happens, I am grateful too, and honoured and never more so than today.'

Something of her mistake begins to occur to her with this word. 'Honoured.' She turns from him and continues on her way along the path. He catches up with her, his stride besides her a confident one and they walk towards the lake and back towards her flat. She is finding it difficult to breathe normally and cannot find anything to say. At the bridge, he stops.

'Can I be a rat and cry off the sherry? I'm not feeling very sociable today.'

Pressing down her questions, she nods and he stoops to kiss her goodnight.

'It is wonderful to have you back again,' he tells her and she makes herself walk away without turning back.

When he has gone, and she is near the flat, it strikes her that, for once, he has not suggested another meeting. Unease starts in the pit of her stomach as she walks home and grows stronger as she chats with their guests. Angela is staying with them and teases her about Ireland and she reassures them that it is not flowing with cream and steaks. Later that evening, all her friends finally gone, she does what she has been longing to do all evening and goes to sit alone in her bedroom. The flat is still, with Alan away somewhere on night duty and Angela in bed. She leaves the lights off, and the curtains open. The night sky is dark, with no moon, and the occasional sudden movement of search lights over the city across the ceiling. Pacing her bedroom floor in the dark, she tries to remember the kind expression on Charles' face as she told him, the polite attention, and the slight puzzlement, and the word 'honoured' terrifies her.

As the night advances, a panic begins to unsettle her even more and, in a restless moment, she walks downstairs to phone Charles' flat, careful not to disturb Angela. The phone rings out and she puts down the receiver and walks back upstairs, frightened at what she has done. The next day, a note arrives from Charles saying he is caught up in work for the next few days but that he will phone her at the weekend, to meet for dinner. He signs it, as always, with love and this reassures her.

As the week advances, she grows more and more uneasy, regretting her confession in the park. Feeling like a spy, she makes a furtive trip past his flat late one evening to see the window darkened. In a dark mood, she walks for an hour or so, feeling the need to do something, make a gesture. Returning home, the silence of her flat is like a reproach to her, the radio in the downstairs flat playing *Carmen*, the sounds of the 'Habanera' driving her to a frenzy. Alan and Angela have left for the cinema and the night looms over her, empty and dull. Suddenly she realises that she cannot spend another night in the darkness, pacing back and forth, wondering where Charles is and what he is feeling. All in an instant she jumps up, throws together a small night case and then sits down to write a letter to Alan. She writes without a pause, not daring to re-read it.

'Dear Alan. I must tell you. I am in love with Charles Ritchie and plan to go and live with him. You must have realised this. I am truly sorry, more than I can say. I'm also sorry to have to tell you this in a letter but it has been so difficult to speak openly. I feel that we cannot go on in this way. I say this as much for your sake as mine. It would not be honest and it would not be fair to any of us. You must also believe me when I tell you how much you mean to me and how grateful I am for you in my life.'

She pauses and then adds:

'In all of our time together, I have never quite known what you wanted me for. I will send for my things next week.'

She goes into his bedroom and leaves the letter on Alan's pillow. Putting on her coat, and fetching her suitcase, she makes her way out into the night, towards Charles' flat. The night is dark, with search lights sweeping down towards the Houses of Parliament, and very few people on the streets. His apartment looks deserted but the caretaker lets her in, telling her that Mr Ritchie went out to dinner towards Whitehall earlier that evening and had just phoned to say there was a raid down there and no one is allowed back for an hour or so. She tells the caretaker that Mr Ritchie is expecting her and he nods impassively and unlocks the door for her.

Leaving her suitcase in the hall, she walks into his empty sitting room and turns on a small lamp, checking first that the blackout curtains are in place. Sitting on his armchair, the first time alone in that room, she thinks of her previous nights there. A moment of terror strikes when she hears the distant wailing of sirens, and the sound of breaking glass nearby, the unsettling idea that Charles might be caught in a raid on this night of all nights. Suddenly restless, she gets up and starts prowling around the room.

She wanders into the bedroom, where suddenly the image comes to her of two heads rearing up from the bed. Charles and Eva. The woman she has never seen. She has never seen Eva but her visible ghost is often before her, never more so that now, in Charles' bedroom? She stoops down towards the pillow and catches the hint of a woman's perfume lingering there. Her own, the violet scent she uses. The vision of the startled lovers seems so real to her and the bedroom feels so airless, so fetid, that she shudders and turns back to the wall to knock off the light. She slams the door shut and walks back into the sitting room to sit and wait.

Around eleven, she hears his key in the landing door and for a moment, she wonders if he is alone. He is. By the guarded look on his face, she guesses that the caretaker has told him she was there.

'Charles,' she begins, 'I'm here to stay', but something in his face makes her stop. It is the same look he had given the fox fur woman in the nightclub. He keeps looking at her intently and she finds herself faltering. His tone when he does finally speak is friendly, but firm.

'Elizabeth. I hope you haven't been waiting too long. I've been at a work dinner. We got caught in a raid. Drink?'

He makes a move to pour her one, careful not to notice her suitcase on the landing outside, in plain sight. She wonders about starting again, pleading with him, but instead finds herself saying,

'No, I'm afraid not. I'm off to stay with Angela in Kent tomorrow and popped in on the off chance, just to say hello.'

Mistakes London 1942

She gets up and he walks her to the door. He grasps her arm.

'I'll phone up next week. Perhaps lunch when you get back?'

'That would be nice.'

He offers to walk her downstairs, but she refuses. No kiss passes between them as she stands on the landing and picks up her suitcase and she hurries out the door and down into the street. At Clarence Terrace she lets herself in, chilled to the bone.

She sleeps little, dozing fitfully until late into the morning. She delays leaving her bedroom until she is sure that Alan is gone. A quick glance around his bedroom reveals no sign of her letter. With her new manuscript to finish, she sits down at her desk and works furiously, preparing some letters for the post. Downstairs, she finds a letter in the post-box from Charles. Delivered by hand. Dreading its contents, she goes out into the sunny day and walks down as far as Regent's Street where, overcome by curiosity, she tears it open.

'My Dear Elizabeth, I wonder if it would be wiser to stop meeting for a time. You know what I am like, woman-wise and, of course, you know all about Eva. I wish I could feel as you do but I'm afraid the truth is that I don't. Also believe me when I say that I'll always be grateful that we met. Charles.'

She stands on Baker Street in the sunshine, busy crowds passing her by, and cries, as she has not cried since she was a girl in Hythe, on that terrible day when she was twelve. She doesn't bother to cover her face, aware of those staring at her, the desolation of those words washing over her as people jostle past her, a well-dressed woman who should know better, making a spectacle of herself in the street. A few stop to frown, a public display of grief in these time a sign of unpatriotic self-indulgence. Unheeding, she takes the note and tears it up, dropping it on the street. Then she makes her way home where Angela is having tea.

'When are you back home?'

'Are you trying to evict me, Elizabeth? This evening, as it happens. I need to see if the place is still standing. Why do you ask?'

'Can you take me for a week or so? I must get these stories finished by the end of the month and London is too noisy. Do say you can squeeze me in?'

Angela looks at her narrowly.

'Alan looked like thunder at breakfast. Is that why? And also what about Charles?'

Elizabeth looks at her.

'I'm afraid things are a little jangled between us now. I told him how I feel about him.'

Angela makes no comment and Elizabeth realises, with something of a lurch in her heart, that Angela doesn't ask what Charles' response was.

Elizabeth breaks the silence.

'Please say yes.'

'Of course you can, Bitha. John is popping in for me at six and so we both can catch a lift with him. Better than dragging that typewriter all the way down to King's Cross.'

At six, when Alan returns, she and Angela are in their travelling coats, their bags ready and for a moment, he looks alarmed. She hurries to explain.

'Alan, I need to get these stories done by the end of the month, Richard is on the warpath and so Angela is taking me in for the duration. I need to get away from London. I'll phone when we get there.'

He looks at her with something nearing astonishment as she goes to kiss him. They hear the toot of a car horn in the street and she hurries out, leaving him standing there, wordless. She doesn't dare to look back at him.

Later that week, the weather turns fine and she takes her breakfast in the garden, her mind wandering, replaying that encounter with

Mistakes London 1942

Charles, and the words of his note drumming in her mind. A memory comes to her, a picture on the wall of her childhood bedroom in Dublin, a baby in a wooden cradle floating smilingly on an immense flood. All around that smiling baby, the tips of submerged trees, houses, cottages. The sight of that baby, unheeding of the imminent potential for disaster, always made her uneasy as a child. Now she feels as if she is imminent danger of being capsized, that she will be tipped into an immense flood. She makes herself stand up and go and begin work, sitting at the wooden table in Angela's small kitchen.

For the next two weeks in the small cottage, the house silent during the day while her hosts are in Oxford, she finishes her stories. Reading her manuscript one afternoon, she thinks, maybe another London story. Pulling the dust sheet off her typewriter, she puts in a sheet of paper and pauses. The day is bright and somewhere nearby tennis is being played, the pock of the balls hitting the racquets comforting. She thinks of her first evening with Charles, the full moon, the deserted London streets, the Park in silver light and suddenly a ragged cough seizes her and she cries, a few ugly, hacking cries, tears forcing themselves down her face. Just as suddenly, it stops and she wipes her face with the palms of her hands.

'Mysterious Kor,' she types.

'At least I have a title,' she thinks. She imagines two lovers wandering the streets of London in the moonlight. One is a young girl, the other a young soldier on leave. All of the pubs are closed and they have nowhere to go. At home in the girl's tiny flat, another young woman, her housemate, a well-behaved girl with flaxen hair, waits for them, too naïve to understand that she should go to bed and give them precious time together. The naïve young woman waits patiently for them, wondering why they are delaying, cocoa cups at the ready while the two young lovers walk aimlessly around the railings of the park, at a loss to find somewhere to make love. In her frustration, the young woman remembers the lost city of Kor, the indestructible city, the city of the dead bathed in moonlight, and starts quoting from it, to the delight of her soldier lover, as they are both very young and the books of their childhood are still real to them. In their yearning for each other, they transform London into an unreal city, a dream world. For the next two days, she writes and she lives with her two lovers, now with names, the enchanting Pepita and the callow, good-natured Arthur, wandering in their magical, dead city of the night, the anticlimax of the return to the tiny flat where the silly, sweet Callie waits for them and where Pepita snubs her and makes her cry.

'You look better,' Angela tells her one evening, over drinks.

'Really,' Elizabeth feels a little surprised. 'I've been working away on these stories. Do you know, I think I'm almost there.'

'Good. Good.' Angela pauses and then asks quickly, shooting her a glance.

'So have you phoned him yet?'

Elizabeth is surprised.

'No, not yet. I think I will give it some time. There may be another woman on the scene, in fact I'm almost sure that there is.'

'I meant Alan. Have you phoned Alan?'

Angela looks annoyed and Elizabeth blushes.

'I am afraid to. Again, I made a terrible blunder there.'

Angela stands up.

'Well, if you won't, I will. I'm going to suggest he come down for the weekend. It's about time.'

By Friday, the story is finished and she types up the final copy, and then, on an impulse, types another. She thinks for a while and then puts it into an envelope. Picking up a postcard, she writes.

'Charles. I thought this story might interest you. Memories of a moonlit night in London. I've called it "Mysterious Kor". Do you remember? All my love E.'

As she seals the envelope, she begins to imagine Charles for the first time in weeks. Sitting at Angela's kitchen table, the sun outside, the sound of someone mowing the grass, she imagines him getting the letter. She knows that at first, seeing the envelope, he will be a little startled at the handwriting. He will be in his flat, perhaps still in his dressing gown, Eva about somewhere or having just left. He will wait until he is alone and then will tear the envelope and be relieved to find the story waiting for him. As he reads, memories of that night will return and, by the end of his reading he will sit for a moment and think. And then he will pick up a pen and begin to write to her.

A car pulls up outside, disturbing her daydream. It is Alan, just arrived from the train station. She stands up to go out and greet him, a smile on her face.

Indian Summer
London
1946

Alan watches as Elizabeth puts down the phone and turns towards him, her face pale. There is an unfamiliar glint in her eyes that begins to worry Alan. He waits for her to speak. After a few moments, she squares her shoulders and bursts into explanation. They are alone but her voice is unnecessarily loud, as if preparing to tell an anecdote at a sherry party. Alan listens with concern.

'That was Charles, Alan. He sends his best. Apparently, it's all been settled. Angela was right. He IS marrying his cousin Sylvia next month in Ottawa.'

Alan marvels at the steadiness of her voice, the deliberate lightness of her tone. He wonders if it would have been better for her to hear the news alone. Angela had never mentioned anything about a wedding, he is sure of that. He grimaces but says nothing. So unnecessary between the two of them after all these years. He can't think of anything to say and so he just stands there and looks at her. She is still holding the phone and he can hear the drone of the line, now dead.

'His cousin. Who would have guessed?'

She laughs but he stays silent. Any expression of approval would be an insult to her.

It is nearly the end of September and London is in the midst of an Indian summer. Even now, in the late afternoon, brilliant sunlight fills their drawing room with a miraculous blaze that seems unending. Around her, beams of light catch the swirl of dust in the air, and give a sheen to the skirt of her crisp town suit. Here and there around the room, reflected gold light burnishes the glass on the paintings and along the windows of the bureau. The warm breeze carries in chatter and the occasional burst of laughter from the park and, with it, the sweet smell of petrol warmed by the sun. As they stand there, Alan watching her intently, this breeze stirs the lace curtain behind Elizabeth, the brilliant light catching the tints of auburn at her temple, her face drawn and pale against the unexpected glowing illumination of her hair.

She looks down at the phone, as if unable to move. Catching her glance, Alan orders her in a firm tone.

'Get your coat, Bitha. We're going for a walk.'

She looks at him gratefully and puts down the phone with a slight crash, knocking it against the ormolu table.

They cross the bridge into the busy park, the promise of unseasonable sunshine drawing families, lovers, and solitary walkers from all over the city, all fleeing offices and shops early, eager to walk in this unexpected paradise of warm September sunshine. The trees are still in full leaf despite the dreary summer, their greenery lush and un-withered, almost transparent in this paler, sharper autumnal light spilling out from the setting sun. Alan leads them towards the Rose Garden where the tall bushes are in full scent, their highest blossom straining upwards into the slant of afternoon sun as if to store up the last of this blessed golden warmth against the remorseless advance of the seasons.

A band can be heard in the distance, the strains of 'Sweet Lass of Richmond Hill'. He frowns and instead nods towards some vacant benches away from the surge of people. They settle themselves down, taking off their coats, their heads still bathed by the bright sunlight, the creeping shadows of evening touching their feet. He says nothing, stealing a glance at her when he thinks he is unnoticed. The band moves on to the 'Habanera' and, with this, she begins to squirm and starts fiddling with her watch. As he sits there, he can feel the bench move as she grows more restless and attempts and fails to light up a cigarette. Something of a panic seems to gradually overtake her as she listens. Alan watches with concern as her eyes begin to dart around the busy park, searching for something, her breath becoming more and more strained. Finally she begins to murmur, as if to herself, not seeing him.

'I need to call him back. I need to go. I can't…I can't.'

She seems to want to stand up and he grips her elbow, forcing her to stay sitting. She collapses back into the bench while he talks to her in a low voice, ignoring the glances of passers-by.

'Steady, Bitha, steady. We need to stay here, just the two of us.'

She looks at him with that same glitter in her eye, not seeming to recognise him and he takes a firm grip of her hand and begins to stroke it with one finger. They sit in silence for a few minutes, to all outward appearances a courting couple, while her breathing gradually returns to normal and he murmurs her name from time to time. Her breath is still coming in short gasps and her colour is bad, but he keeps a hold of her hand. The light shifts as the sun begins to set behind the trees, but, somehow, they are still in direct sunlight, as the crowds around them begin to thin out. A burst of applause signals the end of the concert. For a few moments, a surge of people pass them by, intent on home and dinner, ignoring the couple holding hands, the distressed looking woman, the older man who keeps murmuring her name.

The silence around them becomes more pronounced and a bird high on a tree above them begins a solitary, assertive song, somehow defiant against the growing darkness. The sun grows brighter, the glare of glowing pink gold more intense, the trees in front of them clearer and clearer in detail. To keep himself calm, Alan thinks of a landscape by Claude Lorrain that he loves in the National Gallery, the highest tree in front of them still bathed in the pink glare of the setting sun, the mellow light making it impossibly beautiful. He looks up and he notices that she has followed his gaze. In this, the harbinger of dusk, they both find their eyes drawn upwards as the light of the sunset gathers above them for a final triumph. For several minutes, they stay sitting there until her breathing returns to normal. It is growing colder, the true complexion of the season revealing itself with the setting sun. Finally Alan breaks the silence.

'Maybe it is time for us to make a move? To leave London.'

She starts at this and he adds.

'Back home, to Cork.'

She looks surprised and he turns towards her.

'Think about it, Elizabeth. Just one home to run. Money to put in a bathroom and fix the roof. None of this fuss here. Time to finish your book.'

'Leave London?' She sounds surprised but willing to listen. The bell is being rung for the park to close and she goes to stand up but he stops her.

'Away from this place. We're getting too old for London.'

As he talks, he realises that she isn't listening, or simply half listening and so he keeps talking, to allow her time to recover. The spectre of her father's final illness, talking himself into hoarseness, has always haunted Alan. She looks at him, taking her hand away from his and then her glance sweeps the familiar scene around her, made newly bereft. It seems to calm her, this idea of leaving London, now haunted by Charles. He thinks this would be for the best, the scenes of her love replaced by the quiet of Bowen's Court. Ever since she met Charles, at the start of the war, she has been in high good looks, or so Alan has thought, her face glowing, her walk bold and confident, while he has felt the ten years between them multiply. As she experienced this new youthfulness, he felt his age more and more, the gap between them widening. More and more in the past year, his sore leg has been making him feel less and less like walking, feeling old and heavy. He hasn't grudged her this, her shining happiness has lightened his life but now, the moment he dreaded has come. In repose, her face looks somehow shrunken, not exactly older but lessened by this news.

Charles always seemed a decent sort, Alan thinks, a considerate man, always pleasant to him and a welcome dinner guest. Over the past five years, they have become friends, Alan likes to think, Charles sometimes dropping into the flat when Elizabeth had been away in Ireland, to talk about the latest news from North Africa or Normandy, sharing a whiskey with him, both of them lonely for her. A decent sort but he wonders at his cruelty. They had met Sylvia, his cousin, when she was in London last year and Charles had brought her to tea. Pretty, very pretty, shy, lady-like, a nice young woman. Nice indeed but hardly Elizabeth. Indeed Elizabeth had been especially kind to her, sending her one of her books, complimenting her on her clothes. That will all stop now, Alan thinks grimly. I suppose a female cousin is never seen as any kind of threat, a kind of sister, rather. Now, from this unexpected quarter, a crippling blow. Alan supposes he should be glad that Elizabeth will not be leaving him now, but he always knew that Charles didn't want her. Elizabeth leaving him for Charles now seems better than Elizabeth left shattered. In the last few minutes it occurs to him that she was always made of sterner stuff than her poor father. She seems to be coming round, and turns to ask him.

'But your new job?'

He makes a face, dismissing that idea. He had been offered a new post with an educational company and she had been in favour of him accepting it but given all the trouble with his knee, he didn't want it.

'Too old to start all that again. I'm tired, old girl. This war took it out of me. We need a rest. You work too hard, you always did.'

They both know that that's not really true. Ever since she met Charles, she has been in splendid looks, and writing like she has never written before. As soon as the idea occurred to him, he knew it was the right thing to do. To leave London. To take refuge at home. All the places around her, this very park, all spent with Charles. To take her away from that to the comfort of the empty fields at home, the long, quiet nights in Bowen's Court.

She takes her hand out of his and places it on his arm, looking directly at him for the first time in a while. Her voice is low and troubled.

'Alan, about that silly letter…I should never…'

He waves his hand to cut her off and stands up.

'Time to get out of here, Bitha. We'll be locked in.'

She stands up and he fusses her into her coat. She shivers slightly.

'You'll catch cold. Here, have you got a hat?'

She searches in her pockets and finds a light scarf, throwing it over her head and tying it firmly. He is sorry to see her hair covered, the scarf making her look even more pinched and worn out in the fading light. They begin to walk slowly towards the open gate, where the attendant is waiting to lock up.

'Yes, I'll write to the landlord tomorrow and tell him that I'm giving notice. We could be *in situ* by the late spring. Get all the furniture back to Bowen's Court and then we can start working on getting the old place in ship shape.'

He keeps talking and she nods because he can't bear to hear her apology about that damned letter and she knows it. That was a killer blow, even though she came back the same night, clearly not wanted by Charles but the letter stung. It still does. He only survived it by reassuring himself that Charles would never marry her. Funny, now that he is proved right, he can take no comfort in it. He is her only option, now that Charles was gone. He had burnt the letter but one phrase sticks in his mind, turning there like a sliver of shrapnel. 'I never knew quite what you wanted me for.' Didn't she? After all these years, how could she ask such a thing?

She nods. They pause to allow a man with a child in a pram to exit the gate and they follow him. As they walk towards Marylebone High Street, a thought strikes her.

'I can't imagine they will have children. Do you?'

He shakes his head, relieved she can begin to talk about it.

'Cousins. Unlikely.'

'Second, I believe.'

'Even worse.'

She laughs.

'Do you know how many Bowens married their cousins? Like the Hapsburgs in that. Queen Victoria married her cousin, didn't she? Look what that led to…the Kaiser!'

She walks ahead, and he pauses before a shop window to light his pipe. A memory comes to him. When they announced their engagement, all those years ago, two of her aunts came over from Dublin and bade him to tea, 'to get to know you, away from Bitha', as their note put it. A discreet meeting in a hotel off Brook Street. Two charming women, full of compliments and welcome but, as the afternoon unfolded, on a mission of some seriousness. He had been nervous of the meeting, not sure how Bitha's family would take the suddenness of their engagement. They were somewhat intimidated by his reputation as an intellectual, or so she told him, with great amusement. Also, she teased him that he was a fortune hunter, with Bowen's Court in his sights, but her father made it clear what a liability the house was.

'I'm afraid it will suck you both dry, when the time comes, my dear boy. It has me,' her father told Alan with a grimace.

Alan was nervous at first in this fussy tea room with her two aunts, afraid of dropping a plate or in some other way ruining his chances of marriage, but they made it plain that they were on his side. It began to worry him that they were perhaps too much so. Despite this, he found himself charmed by their sweetness, their obvious fondness for Elizabeth, their sincere desire to make their good will towards him known. It was only towards the end of tea, almost as an afterthought, that their real intention became obvious.

One aunt, Myra, the married one, took it upon herself to bring it up. To her credit, she did so with admirable tact. Myra had been toying with a tiny éclair and put down her fork with some regret and dabbed her mouth with the stiff napkin with decision.

'My dear Alan, if I may call you that?'

He nodded eagerly.

'So sweet. You are family now and you must call me Aunt Myra. Alan, this is a delicate matter.'

She paused and he was at a loss. Were they worried about money?

'Well, our darling Bitha. With no mother and her dear father as he is, she is very special to us, isn't she Laura?'

The other aunt, unmarried, quieter, radiantly pretty in a kind of old-fashioned way, deferred to her more energetic sister-in-law, a wife and a matron and used to giving orders. Nevertheless Laura also put down her tea cup, as a gesture towards the seriousness of the moment. With that, Aunt Myra looked around the crowded room before lowering her voice.

'You will be the man of the family.'

Alan liked this idea of himself as the man of the family.

'It is best we tell you ourselves… Well, to be blunt, our darling girl really isn't suited to motherhood. There, I've said it.'

The subject broached, Aunt Myra looked relieved and it was Alan's turn to look uncomfortable, trapped in this pretty place, a backwater of Victorian respectability. The first breech made in the wall of silence, Aunt Myra was unstoppable now.

'Marriage is the right path for Elizabeth. Emphatically yes, especially to an intellectual. Such a bright girl and so original, and her art work, so clever. You will be an admirable…', she took her time looking for the right word, 'companion for her. Yes, companion. But babies and so forth, well no. Quite out of the question. Do promise me?'

Having delivered herself of her difficult message, Aunt Myra beamed at him and Alan found himself wishing to be far away from these sweet charming women at this polite tea table. Unfortunately some hot cakes arrived, to their delight, and he was trapped. He slipped away for a moment, pleading a work phone call, and sat for a few moments in the cloakroom wondering if he could just slip away.

When he had received this invitation and Elizabeth had urged him to go, the idea, however discreetly managed, of discussing his life with Elizabeth never crossed his mind. In this polite temple of femininity, it was excruciatingly embarrassing. As if he hadn't worried about it already, in the dark of the night and now here were her aunts prepared to discuss it openly, making it clear that he must be a husband but no husband. It bothered him that such a worldly woman should have intuited that she could talk openly to him like this.

When he returned to the table, the hot cakes had all been dispatched and he began to make his excuses to leave. This need to leave became acute when Aunt Laura began to reminisce, much to Aunt Myra's discomfort.

'That young man in Italy. What was his name? John something? No, he would have been unsuitable, always passionate and impulsive, or so one always felt. Undeniably handsome and dashing, but much the wrong choice for her.'

She lowered her voice and dabbed her mouth with her napkin. Emboldened by his silence, Aunt Myra rushed in, anxious to re-establish her authority and end this conversation.

'Yes, indeed, I insisted that she return him the engagement ring. She was quite put out with me but, now…'

Aunt Myra looked wistful.

'He was terribly cut up, you know. John…John…, yes John Lesworth. I knew I'd remember.'

Aunt Myra looked slightly annoyed at her sister-in-law. Elizabeth had told him that her Aunt Myra was the most efficient woman she knew when it came to gardening, servants and the management of her children and the nearest thing she had ever had to a mother.

'Yes, I put an end to it and I have been proved right. But enough about that, Laura, we didn't invite dear Alan hear to hear all of those ancient tales.'

She glared at her sister-in-law who had taken refuge in some orange chocolate cake, but before she did, Laura flashed back.

'Hardly ancient, Myra dear, it was only last year.'

Only last year. Alan had heard of this earlier suitor, mentioned casually by Elizabeth as an episode of romantic folly when she lived in Italy but clearly it was more important and more recent, with an engagement ring. Aunt Laura's words stung. Impulsive. Passionate. Handsome. There was clearly no limit to the humiliation he would have to endure in this tea room this afternoon. The lack of all of these qualities in him would save Elizabeth from the temptations of motherhood.

'Now, Laura, as I keep saying but you don't seem to be listening, Bitha has met Alan and now all of that is ancient history.'

Her sister-in-law suitably chastened, Aunt Myra returned to her quarry.

'But no children. You must ensure that, dear Alan. You are the older and of course so sensible and wise, we can all see that. You will be her ideal companion. That's why we are so pleased to see you in the family. You are already one of us. Is he not, Laura?'

The dangerous words spoken, the other aunt joined in, nodding happily.

'Besides, with the Bowens and all that intermarriage.'

The two aunts, neither of them born a Bowen and so safe from genetic contagion, nodded with authority and a sense of safety.

'Not at all a good idea. I think her dear mother would have approved, wouldn't she, Laura?'

Having slapped her down, Aunt Myra needed her to copper fasten this deal.

'So dear, you do agree?'

He nodded, unable to speak, but there was a clear nod. All of them were anxious to leave after that, the women pleading pressing engagements with the dressmakers for the wedding.

Later that day, when Elizabeth asked him how it had all gone, he told her 'swimmingly' and she laughed and said they were relieved to get her off their hands and that he should know that. Somehow, that rasped his nerves, anxious as he was to marry her and afraid that she would change her mind. Somehow, he never could like Aunt Myra, much as he tried, in the years since. When he and Elizabeth started their lives together, he bore the warnings in mind and it made their first few months so much easier. By the time she inherited Bowen's Court, all talk of an heir had stopped. Now, he is not so sure. Would it have been a good thing? Would it have saved her from this moment of utter loss? Would she have wanted a child with Charles?

The air has grown colder and so he motions to her that they should leave. She still looks a little unsettled to him and so, despite his sore knee, he suggests they walk down towards Regent's Street. She takes her time, slowing her rapid stride to his shuffle and they cross into Hanover Square and down Brook Street where he stops before Claridge's.

'Sherry?' he asks her.

She looks down at her coat.

'Will we pass muster like this?'

Alan feels the need to sit down, his knee sore.

'We'd better. I need a drink.'

Alan remembers walking past this hotel, a year ago, and catching a glimpse of Elizabeth sitting inside, her book abandoned, her gaze distant. He had lingered for a moment to look at her, caught in her own private dream world, and hurried on, knowing that she was waiting for Charles. He nods. Time to lay those ghosts to rest.

At the door, he pauses.

'I can't remember. Was this where I met your aunts, back in '22, for the big interview? Or was it the Savoy?'

She has taken off her scarf and paused to pat down her hair in front of the large mirror.

'What a peculiar thing to remember. I had forgotten all about that. They were charmed with you, that I do recall. Still are.'

She looks at him, her colour better than it had been in the park.

'You can ask Aunt Myra if it was here. We are seeing her in Dublin next month and you know how she is. Nearly seventy-seven and remembers everything. I tell her, she should have been the writer but, you know she only pretends to read my books.'

He stays where he is, standing in the hall. She waits, anxious for her drink, wondering at his hesitation but unwilling to move him on. He decides to keep talking.

'Yes. I think it was here. Bit of an ordeal, as I remember it. Quite a grilling from Myra and your Aunt Laura warned me against the dangers of us ever having children.'

She looks a little shocked. People are walking past, an elderly lady sitting in earshot. Her face grows pale again.

'You never told me that. What were they thinking?'

She stops, then starts again.

'Aunt Laura? Are you sure? I can't imagine her talking about anything like that with a man?'

He glares at her.

'Of course I'm sure. Would I make it up?'

She nods.

'Of course you wouldn't. But you never told me at the time. I'm quite sure you didn't.'

'Didn't I? I thought I had. I suppose they thought they were doing the right thing.'

He pauses and then plunges onwards. This day is as good as any to ask. The thought had tormented him for years. He asks her straight out, all his doubt in his face.

'Was it the right thing, Bitha?'

Indian Summer London 1946

She looks at him, wordless, staring, and he is dismayed at the thought of this conversation between them, twenty-five years too late. He should have asked her then. Not now. Not when it is too late.

She begins to say something but, for once, is caught up in a stammer...

'm...m....'

'Leave it, old girl. Too many shocks for one day.'

He limps away into the bar, leaving her behind, unable to look at her, standing there, unwilling to talk any further. He knows that she is as horrified as he is, contemplating the possibility of the child they could have had together.

'Two sherries,' He tells the bar man.

The aunts were only doing what they thought was best, he tells himself, but oh, what had they taken from him and Elizabeth. Robert, if it was a boy, to keep the Bowen line in order. Florence, if a girl. The first visit to Bowen's Court, the bundle of shawls being taken carefully out of the car. Waiting in the cold winter air for the young boy or girl, at the bridge in Stephen's Green, a dark blue gabardine coat, hand being held by the governess as they walk for afternoon tea in the Shelbourne. The third at their side in their travels in Italy, the small bed in the hotel bedroom, the smaller chair at table in the Italian loggia. The tears of the first journey to school, the new suitcases and trunk, Bitha crying on the bed upstairs when the car had left. The family heirloom being handed over for the coming-of-age birthday, jokes to relieve the emotion of the moment as the watch is presented, the pearls slipped around the young neck. The young man or woman being told about the trees at Bowen's Court, the possibility of reclaiming some of the land, the selling of some stocks to refurbish the house. The shining idea of a future being reflected in those impatient young eyes, half-listening as they plan for the survival of the house. Alan sees it all as he orders their drinks and takes his first sip of sherry. He dare not turn around and look for Elizabeth. For all he knows, she is still standing in the hallway of the hotel, fixing her hair in the mirror, a fixed smile on her face, made pale again.

Happy Autumn Fields
Cork
September 1947

Elizabeth sits at her desk, her unfinished manuscript in front of her and stares at it in despair. She thinks to herself, 'my father was driven mad writing a book he couldn't finish. And now it's my turn.' She remembers that terrible day in her childhood when he burst into the Dining Room, startling her mother and herself, his face flushed, his eyes glittering, his manuscript held aloft in his hands. Without a word, he flung it out of the open windows into the street below in one wild thrust. She wondered if he would follow his manuscript out the window and she looked at her mother in terror, to see the same terror on her mother's gentle face. He stood there looking out for a moment and his laugh as he watched the papers swirling around in the wind outside was somehow worse than the days of brooding silence that had preceded it. While he laughed, she and her mother sat frozen in their chairs, until finally Elizabeth stood up to go to her father. At this, her mother also got up, took a firm hold of her hand to keep her still, not letting go as she turned to phone the doctor. Now, forty years later, her own unfinished manuscript lies beside her on the desk and she wonders if a moment will come when she stands up to fling it out the window, when Alan will phone the doctor and have her taken away like her father, pressed forever into melancholy.

It is early September in north Cork, heavy and airless, with dark clouds threatening in the skies over the newly mown demesne. Elizabeth sits waiting, as they all do, for the weather to break, but the rain doesn't come, leaving the countryside panting and arid. Instead of writing, she stares out of the window, the autumn fields outside as familiar to her as her own face in the mirror and wonders at her folly in leaving London. The novel she is expected to complete is now a torment to her, the manuscript a reproach whenever she glances at it. Downstairs, her husband is waiting patiently to have his first secret drink of the day, a drink that is secret to no one. Their permanent move back to Cork has become a rapid slide into old age for Alan. Almost overnight, the capable man who managed the dismantling of their London life with such speed, is dwindling into a bewildered invalid, looking to her with increasing irritation, wondering where his life has gone.

As she sits there, watching the harvest fields from her window, she thinks, 'Somewhere in Paris, the man I love with all my being is preparing to get married.' The thought of that marriage is like shrapnel in her breast. And so, for now, all she can do is dream of London.

London. Her lost home overlooking Regent's Park. She thinks of London constantly as she watches the tractors pass by laden with hay, the random flight of birds across the sky, the rooks massing in the trees furthest away from the house. There is a hint of premature autumn on the leaves, a slight change in the light in the evenings and she dreads the coming of winter. To ward it off, she dreams of the early years of the war in London, the feverish anticipation of Charles' visits, in a city transformed by moonlight. All of this lurks in the manuscript,

Happy Autumn Fields Cork September 1947

ready to bite her and so she occupies herself with other tasks, reviews, letters, essays, anything but the story of her siren years in London with Charles. His image has entwined itself around her mind, her heart, and most of her thoughts. For the first time in her life, to write her novel is a torment she cannot face. To be alone in her room with her typewriter is to have the image of Charles most keenly in front of her, reminding her of her loss, and yet it is the only room in the house where she can be left in peace for most of the morning.

Each scene from those years is as fresh as if it were yesterday but, with the breaking up of the flat and the dismantling of her life there, in the last week, she found herself in a nightmare of renewed longing for Charles. On her last night in the flat in London, lying on the bed where they had spent so much time together, she broke her resolve and phoned him in Paris, yearning to hear his voice. Instead Sylvia answered and Elizabeth found herself cursing her out loud and slamming down the phone.

In the mornings, Alan spends hours moving around the Library, ostensibly settling his books and papers, in reality waiting for his first whiskey. At lunch, he complains to her about all he has to do, more and more impatient with the shortcomings of the house. Although it was his idea to move back here, he rails at the damp in the house, the lack of proper bathrooms, the dismal indoor light in the winter and the overpowering heat of the summer. Some evenings, the two of them alone, Teresa lying low in the kitchen, he rants away over dinner and she sits there nodding and smiling and waiting for him to stop, as he inevitably does. This time at her desk is her refuge from his bewildered anger, and his gusts of rage towards her, and towards the rest of the world.

September passes slowly, the rain stays away and still the novel lies on her desk. It is nearly finished, and it could be good, possibly her best, but she cannot bear to write. She sits down every morning with resolution but the hopelessness of it overwhelms her. She looks out her window and thoughts of Charles twist inside her and drive her to work furiously on anything but fiction. It strikes her that thoughts of Charles dominate her daily life, just as her writing used to. On her worst mornings, she stops herself from picking up the phone and ringing him. She succeeds, her fingers on her left hand gripping the back of her right hand until it hurts.

Letters come asking about the progress of the book, and she doesn't answer. Then her publisher phones her politely to ask about the novel, telling of the great interest in New York and the possibility of substantial advances there. 'Dollars, Elizabeth, precious dollars. Think of all you could do with those dollars. New bathrooms for Bowen's Court.' She is afraid Alan will hear this and hurries the publisher off the phone, pleading a domestic crisis. Before she rings off, she promises him that she will have a draft by the end of September. She thinks, 'How can I bear to reread it?'

At night, Elizabeth falls into exhausted sleep and dreams of falling out of high windows, of her father's triumphant laughter as he flings his life's work out of the window, and awakes sobbing, imagining the moans of delight as Charles and his new wife make love. Night after night, his words on the phone echo again, his deep voice casual, a tremor of nervousness betraying him, the words that changed her life. 'Elizabeth. I wanted you and Alan to hear my good news first. Sylvia has done me the kindness of agreeing to marry me.'

Sylvia. His cousin. That quiet, pretty girl, the one Elizabeth had befriended. Each word Charles spoke on the phone to her has now lodged in her chest, almost like a living presence. Slowly over time, each word has flattened out to form a thin film of cutting steel right against her heart. It keeps her awake in the middle of the night, prodding her to remember whenever she forgets, a living wound that torments her. In the early light of morning, as if accidentally touching a severed limb, the sensation of pain wakens her and she is gripped with the nightmarish visions of Charles and of Sylvia, their lovemaking a direct reproach. All of their times together and all of his admiration evaporate in the early hours of the morning, when she lies awake, her arms folded around herself to soothe that thin sheet of steel pressing against her heart, driving her towards despair.

Once, after a particularly difficult night, she wakes in the dim light before dawn, fear gripping her and she thinks, his marriage must be happening around now. Pacing her room as the dawn breaks, she gets up early to attempt to start work on her novel but all she can type is one sentence. 'My father was driven mad by a book he could not finish, and this is now my turn.' She looks at it, and then tears the sheet from the typewriter and rips the paper to pieces.

Letters and phone calls come with invitations to dinner elsewhere and friends asking to come and stay but she puts them all off, pleading the necessity to finish the novel. What she dreads most is the casual moment in a dinner party when some stray fact about Charles emerges, to torment her anew. Arthur comes over to help Teresa pick fruit and she can see he is uneasy with the atmosphere in the house, Alan angry and impatient, and herself shut up at her desk in the mornings and then locked away in her bedroom most afternoons. She finds she cannot be with the child, her attention gone to pieces, and she knows that he is puzzled, wondering if he has done something wrong.

Then, suddenly, a letter arrives from Charles, post-marked Paris. As she comes down to lunch, she catches sight of it on the hall table and her heart lurches and the thin sheet of steel twists at the sight of his handwriting. She stands over it, willing herself not to open it. The front door is open and the scent of roses overhanging the porch is suddenly intoxicating, carried in by a momentary gust of warm air. She remembers Charles saying how he always associated Bowen's Court with the memory of that scent. Some instinct of self-preservation tells her to leave the letter there. During lunch, Alan and Teresa say nothing about it, but, of course they know it is there and who has written it.

All during the afternoon, she busies herself with jam making down in the kitchen, helping Arthur and Teresa, forcing herself not to run upstairs and tear it open. Another few words from Charles, the wrong few, and she fears a collapse. The long agony of this autumn has worn her sanity thin. During dinner, she feels that the entire house is watching the unopened letter on the hall table. At bedtime, she wonders again about taking it up to read but instead she goes up and falls asleep, exhausted by the tension of waiting.

She wakes suddenly in the middle of the night, and gets up and walks downstairs. At the turn of the stairs, she stands, the moonlight flooding the empty hall with a blinding whiteness. Below her she can see the letter on the hall table, caught in a bar of silver from the window over the porch. She stands there looking down and wonders if the summer has been leading to this. A slow, steady unravelling of her peace of mind, her sanity being chipped away by her hourly tormented thoughts of Charles, a fate awaiting her from the moment she saw him four years ago in the church in Kent.

She walks along the hall and picks up the letter, and takes it unopened into the Library. Through a half opened curtain, moonlight lights up the room as she pushes the door open and she walks to the window, the letter in her hand and wonders about simply tearing it up, releasing herself from her misery, and throwing it out the window. She pushes up the window and the rush of cold night air makes her shiver. The fields outside are drenched with moonlight, each tree in the demesne clearly outlined in the blinding light. Nearby, something glints momentarily, a pair of eyes, nothing human, caught in the glare of the moon. A cat, or a fox, she wonders, or a ghost from the past, some dispossessed soul caught in an eternal rage against the Big House. She turns her back on the window to look into the eyes of her ancestors looking down at her and wants to ask them. Had they been caught like her, bound on this wheel of fire? She wonders if they resent her, for taking back the winter house they had reigned in for so many years. She thinks, here in this blanched room, I am the shade and they are the living.

Looking down at the letter, made ghostly by the night time, she begins to imagine the words that will deliver her from her agony. 'My Dearest Elizabeth. I have made a terrible mistake. In her arms, I think only of you and I will return to you as soon as I can. Forgive me for breaking both our hearts. I am returning to you. My Darling, My Darling, My Darling, your devoted Charles.' With this comfort, she puts it back on the hall table and makes her way back up to bed. For the next week, it stays there unopened, always at the top of the pile of incoming mail, and Elizabeth wonders if it is Teresa who keeps putting it there. Not Alan surely.

In the afternoons, the house is stagnant and airless in the September torpor, clouds like weighty blankets cutting off any redeeming light, a kind of grey and the sounds of harvesting coming through the open windows. She goes to her bedroom and takes her clothes off and tries to remember her times with Charles beside her in this bed. All she sees is the two of them conjoined, Charles and Sylvia, their lovemaking an active proof of his rejection of her, all the memories of his body now a torment, a loss, an exile. She examines her body in the long mirror and tries to remember his praise, his delight, but all she sees is Sylvia, younger, blond, pretty. While in bed, she takes out their wartime letters and reads, in a vain attempt to recover that lost time and marvels at her poise in each letter.

Her publisher writes again, pressing for a date of completion and hinting that the advance of five hundred pounds, which she has already used to pay off her taxes, might now be in question. Carelessly she leaves this letter unanswered, then, even worse, she leaves it behind her in the Library one evening. Alan pushes his way into her bedroom the following morning, and her heart sinks when she sees the letter flapping in his hand. As a rule, he never interrupts her morning work, and one glance at the typewriter tells him that she has being doing nothing, which enrages him even more.

'Is this true?' he demands to know.

'Is what true?' she looks up at him, his face reddened by anger, knowing exactly what he wants to know and attempting to parry the blow.

He waves the publisher's letter in her face.

'They want their money back. Five hundred pounds, Elizabeth. We can't afford that. Last week, Richard wrote and told me that you've missed another deadline with the new book.'

She puts her head into her hands. How can she stop him shouting at her?

'Alan. I can't. It's impossible. I can't finish this book. It's too cruel. You, of all people, must understand.'

He stands over her desk, his face caught in the full glare of the morning light, his anger painting his face a brick red. For a moment she remembers him, the tall thin elegant soldier she met at Angela's party, impossibly well read or so it seemed to her and her delight when he seemed interested in her and not the prettier, more confident Angela. He talked to her about books, about the new French writer he was reading, and to her delight, he asked if he could take her to

Happy Autumn Fields Cork September 1947

tea. Later that year, in what seemed a sudden rush, he asked her to marry him, and she didn't hesitate. She thought, 'Aunt Myra will be relieved', and she was relieved herself. Now, twenty years later, that young man was long vanished. Instead there is this Alan, looming over her, his right eye red and inflamed, shouting at her.

'Of course you can. You've been writing for twenty years, it is second nature to you. I refuse to accept this.'

Somewhere behind the bluster she knows there is fear, his fear of seeing her like this.

She looks up at him, and something in her expression seems to unsettle him.

'I've been burnt. Can't you see…every time I start to work on it, I see…I'll go mad like every Bowen who got shut up here.'

He looks helpless, and suddenly afraid and he turns on his heel, his voice breaking with panic.

'This is the limit! I will phone Richard now. I can't bear to see you being put under such pressure.'

When she looks up, Alan is gone, thumping down the stairs. Worried about what he might do when he feels threatened, she follows him down. He is standing in the Library, a glass on the table in front of him, his expression more concentrated than she has seen in a while, on the phone.

'Look, hear. I don't care what meeting Richard is in. Do you understand? Get him to the phone right away, young lady. Tell him this is a matter of urgency. Alan Cameron.'

Elizabeth moves over to take the phone from him but Alan shrugs her away, a little roughly.

'Richard. Alan here. Now what's all this about Elizabeth and the new book? I won't have her bullied, do you hear, not even by an old pal like you? Her health can't stand it, old boy.'

The Last Day at Bowen's Court

Elizabeth frowns at him, to try and make him stop and catches the murmur of Richard's deep voice on the phone, no doubt exercising his usual tact, annoyed to be caught by a drunken belligerent husband in the middle of a busy morning. Whatever he is saying seems to be taking effect, as Alan's expression grows quieter.

'Of course, old man. Never believed you would. But you know Bitha, how hard she works. Damn it all, she needs to rest and build up her strength. This move has been hell for her.'

Elizabeth holds out her hand to take the phone. Alan needs to escape from the blunder he has made. She would prefer not to talk to Richard directly but this seems the lesser of two evils now.

'Richard, my dear. So sorry to have bothered you this morning.'

'Elizabeth. Lovely to hear your voice.'

He sounds relieved, glad to have Alan off his back.

'I was just saying to Alan, we must have you and Blanche over this autumn. Would October suit? I should have that work done for you by then and Alan can show you all the miracles he has wrought with the Library here.'

His kind voice down the line is reassuring. 'October would be heavenly, my dear. You know how much we love Bowen's Court in all its autumn splendour. I'll put Blanche on alert and she can settle dates with you.'

He sounds relieved. October. She has promised. Alan looks at her hopefully and she cannot bear to see the hope in his eyes. Of course she won't be finished by October.

'Wonderful, I am pleased, my dear.'

'Must pop. Shan't keep you from the writing.'

She puts the phone down and turns to give Alan a light kiss on the cheek, stroking his jacket. He looks a little unsettled and rubs his eye. She turns and makes her way back upstairs.

Happy Autumn Fields Cork September 1947

A moment later, Teresa puts her head around the door.

'Will I bring up a bit of lunch for you now?'

'Oh, don't bother about me, Teresa, I'll come down for coffee in an hour or so, you and Alan go ahead and eat without me.'

Instead of going away, Teresa walks over to the desk and looks at the manuscript of the novel.

'Is this the new one, the one about London and the war?'

Elizabeth wants to snatch it away from her.

'Oh that. Well, it's not quite up to scratch. I don't think I've quite managed it.'

'So when will it be done?'

Teresa never asks about a book. Elizabeth finds herself getting a little short-tempered with her.

'I don't imagine it will. I'm tired of it, to tell the truth.'

'That's not like you…not to finish something. You're like your grandfather, the old master. He was a demon for work.'

Elizabeth laughs, a little unsteadily.

'Yes and he went mad in the end. Maybe that's where I'm headed.'

Teresa looks shocked.

'Don't talk nonsense, girl. You're like your mother's people. Look at Mrs Fisher. Tough.'

Yes, Aunt Myra is indestructible but, oh Teresa, I've been so foolish.'

Teresa comes over and stands by her, waiting for her to finish.

'All my eggs in one basket and now they are broken.'

Teresa says nothing, for a minute or two, the sound of mowing coming from the open window, her breathing a little laboured. Then she pats her on the shoulder. Looking down at the manuscript, she says, in a light, almost inconsequential tone.

'Couldn't you finish that book and then send it to him? He'd want to read it, he couldn't help himself.'

Elizabeth looks at her, surprised at what she seems to be suggesting. 'He's married now, for all I know.'

'Well, you were married when he first took up with you. That didn't stop him and it won't stop him now. Go down and read that letter and then finish your book.'

It is Elizabeth's turn to be shocked by Teresa, a devout Catholic, married happily and widowed early.

She turns to go but pausing at the door, takes a sterner tone.

'Anyway, didn't they pay you for it, so now you owe them the book?'

Two days later, Angela arrives unexpectedly, much earlier than she had promised, with some implausible tale about her travel plans gone awry. She stands on the porch of Bowen's Court and chatters on, happily bending over to smell the climbing roses just next to the door.

'You know how impossible Myra is and so when she decamped to Oxford, I was told to make shift where I could, more or less evicted without an excuse and so here I am like a bad penny, throwing myself at your mercy. Anyway I can help Diana and John with all the wedding fuss.'

Charles' letter is sitting on the hall table and Elizabeth can see Angela glance at it as they walk in, but she says nothing and keeps on chatting. Elizabeth imagines that she has been summoned by Alan and this makes Elizabeth very uneasy. Alan is delighted to see Angela but dogs her every step. Elizabeth guesses that Angela has news of Charles for her and know that she must face that. The following afternoon, Angela asks Elizabeth to come for a walk, the habitual heavy grey clouds of this endless September momentarily lifted, a fresh breeze blowing in the open front door. Alan is uneasy, wanting to join them, fussing them about shoes and coats and possible rain, but he is not up to such a walk and they leave him behind on the porch, staring at them until they are out of sight.

Happy Autumn Fields Cork September 1947

By agreement, they set off along the main driveway towards the village. The harvest is in, the fields shorn to a beautiful blond stubble, hedgerows are overgrown and lush and the ground underneath crunches as they stride along. Elizabeth carries an old Alpine stick belonging to her grandfather and swipes at high-standing nettles and thistles left behind by the mower, which gives her a great deal of satisfaction. In front of them, rooks peck at the earth and then rear up at the sound of their approach, the light rays of sun glinting on their dark wings and Elizabeth feels a momentary stirring in her chest, the heavy weight of Charles' words somehow lifting for a moment.

'Seems a shame to waste this delicious fresh air, Bitha, I hardly slept last night with the heat.'

After a moment, she asks,

'And how are you sleeping? You look a little washed out?'

Elizabeth looks at her, wondering how much she should say. The letter is still on the hall table, unopened.

'So my suspicions are correct. Alan sent for you.'

Angela laughs, but avoids her eyes and they fall into silence, a long afternoon ahead, neither anxious to begin.

They take a side path towards the churchyard, pushing their way through the overgrown bushes, and swatting away the flies. As she walks, Elizabeth realises that Charles has become a kind of fever to her, an illness that waxes and wanes with each day. Today she is determined to walk it off, the day warm and bright, a welcome breeze coming down from the Ballyhouras smarting against her face, determined to sweat it out of her system if she can.

'So are you writing? Or blocked, as they say?'

'I am not short of inspiration, dear. Rather the reverse. Inspiration is overwhelming me.'

Angela reaches over and presses her elbow. At this point they reach the church and Elizabeth, catching sight of the overgrown graves, feels a reluctance to continue. Steeling herself, she makes her way over to her father's plot and stands there looking at it. It has been a while since she was there and it looks untidy. She bends down to settle an overturned flower pot.

'This needs a good cleaning, I'll bring Arthur down tomorrow. Or maybe not. He does get spooked in graveyards, the lamb, although he would hate hearing me say it. He's getting to be such a tall boy, I keep having to remind myself that he is only twelve.'

She straightens up and catches Angela looking at her a little anxiously.

'Darling, let's go on towards the mill, I can't bear the dead today.'

As they walk, Elizabeth knows that it is only a matter of time until Angela will talk about Charles. As a child, Angela frightened her with her directness, and one of the worst moments of her life came with her series of questions one quiet afternoon in their bedroom in Aunt Myra's about her dead mother. Now, she feels something of the same mood in Angela, another round of interrogation, but somehow, now it doesn't intimidate her. In a curious way, she welcomes it, painful as it might be. Somehow she trusts Angela now.

They make their way in silence out of the church and retrace their steps into the harvested fields, the reassuring sound of crunching stubble beneath their feet the only noise in the deserted landscape. The fresh wind in their faces whips them on as they gain more and more ground. Soon, Bowen's Court is far below them, the house and the walled garden now swallowed up by the surrounding land, hidden by trees. At the sight of a fallen log, she murmurs, 'Oh Angela, I'm done in' and stops to sit there. The heat of the afternoon suddenly has become too much for her and she slumps down on to the log, to lie there. Suddenly the prospect of her years ahead in this place, in this house, Alan growing more and more discontented, the absence

Happy Autumn Fields Cork September 1947

of Charles growing more powerful the older she gets, overwhelms her as she lies there. She is aware of Angela standing over her, blocking out the sun and squints up to look at her. Her expression is a curious one, both sympathetic and also puzzled.

'Oh, Bitha? How can you let him have so much power over you? You know that he was still seeing Eva up to very recently, don't you?'

She rolls over on the ground, Angela now a giant over her. She glances up at Angela, a sudden feeling of relief within her breast.

'No, I didn't. But Sylvia…'

Angela makes a dismissive gesture.

'You are making much too much of this marriage with Sylvia. He has to get married, all ambassadors must be married, even the pansies. That's the convention. And you know Sylvia. She's a mouse. She won't rattle the cage at all, probably grateful for the chance to play the ambassadress.'

Her voice carries around this deserted landscape, echoing downwards, and Elizabeth listens with a kind of pained fascination.

'I believe Eva's parents intervened. Gladys told me that, knows her through work. Mummy and Daddy back in Boston thought him a fortune hunter, which, to be fair, he isn't.'

Angela keeps up this stream of worldly gossip, with an undercurrent of spite that is completely unlike her. Elizabeth is not sure she believes her, knowing her to be fond of Charles. Elizabeth then forces herself to ask.

'So, w…w…w…when exactly will it take place?'

Angela looks uncomfortable but braces herself to answer.

'Monday, I believe. Two days from now.'

In the silence that follows, Elizabeth looks around, as if trying to escape.

'Forget him, Darling. You must.'

With one movement, Elizabeth rises from the ground and grabs her walking stick.

'Time to head back, I suspect. Alan will call out the Guards if we don't show up soon.'

The next morning, she marches out to the walled garden, scythe in hand and begins to attack the armies of large, luscious nettles choking the lavender beds, while Teresa watches her anxiously from the kitchen, taking care not to be noticed. She ignores her, slashing and chopping, beginning to feel an agreeable sweat on her brow and along her arms and after a few minutes, without asking her, Arthur comes out to help, raking up the weeds and bearing them away on a barrow, happy to be of use. They labour in silence, attacking the worst of the weeds with vigour and as soon as she catches his eye, Arthur begins chatting happily giving her all the local village gossip that he has been longing to tell her, telling her of the new school he will attend next month and all the books they had to buy in Cork city.

'I even saw two of yours there. I wanted to buy one but Mam said it was too hard for me to read. It's called *The House in Paris*. Do you make them too hard so that children won't be able to read them?'

She pushes the hair from her brow and laughs.

'Well not exactly, but that one does have children in it, as a matter of fact.'

'Then I might read it next year,' he tells her, after thinking about it for a moment.

That morning, she works until her hands have grown red and she and Arthur have cleared away the worst of the nettles and the lavender now liberated gives an overpowering scent to accompany their work. She pulls at ropes of greenery, her hands now slick with sweat and shows Arthur.

'Bindweed.'

Happy Autumn Fields Cork September 1947

'What's that?' he asks.

She shows him the long thin ropes of weed she has dragged out.

'It is our enemy, Arthur. Look how it chokes up the gooseberry bushes.'

His face is serious and flushed in the sunlight and, once again, she admires its perfect lines, the shaped eyebrows, and the cheekbones. His face could have been painted by an Egyptian master craftsman, she thinks, and she reminds herself that she has been neglecting him.

'I need to fix up the churchyard, as well, Arthur. Can you lend me a hand?'

He looks delighted with the task.

The following day, Monday as she keeps trying to forget, Elizabeth brings him down to the churchyard in the early morning, as the birds fly overhead on their way to pick over the autumn fields. The day is warm already but the graveyard is sheltered by the high trees and still in shade and sprinkled with the remains of the dew. She begins by dragging out some tools from the shed behind the vestry and Arthur stands over her father's grave while she clears away as much of the growth as possible and sends him to fetch water. He is nervous in the graveyard, always staying close to her side as she crosses over and back to dump the weeds and water the potted plants. At one point, he stops to read the inscription on her father's grave.

'Did I know him, Mrs Cameron?'

'Not really, Arthur. You were a baby when he died. Although he did hold you at your christening but you couldn't possible remember that. He said you looked like trouble…and he was right. My father was always right.'

She looks at his quiet dignified grave and thinks again of his reddened face as he threw all of his papers out the window. Always courteous in public, he had filled their private life with anxiety and tension and she and her mother had fled to Kent without any real regret.

Arthur moves over to the grave of her Aunt Sarah, next to her father.

'And this is your mother?'

'No, my aunt, my father's sister. My m…m…m…,' she begins to stammer and takes a grip of herself…, 'My mother is buried in Kent, where she died.'

'Were you there?'

'Yes, I was, as it happens. On the very day. They didn't allow me to attend and so Angela, Mrs Banks, you know, my cousin, the lady up at the house with us, she and I stayed at home under the care of a very unpleasant old woman, a neighbour. We were inspecting her elegant fox fur when she pounced on us and gave us both a sharp slap on the wrist. We cried for nearly an hour but I think we were relieved to have something else to cry about.'

Arthur listens without emotion, intent of finding out as much as he can. Elizabeth is not sure she can manage too many more of these questions.

'How old were you?'

'About your age.'

She wonders how she can stop all this talk about dead parents when they both turn to hear the sounds of footsteps, the crunch of gravel. A young couple come around the corner into the churchyard and the woman exclaims when she sees Elizabeth kneeling there.

'Elizabeth! What luck?'

The young woman frees herself from the arm of her companion and comes over to hug her.

'Diana, Darling, what are you doing here? John?'

The young man kisses her and shakes hands with Arthur, which delights the boy.

The young woman frowns at her in mock anger.

Happy Autumn Fields Cork September 1947

'Really! You simply can't have forgotten.'

She had. This young couple, her neighbours, were getting married the following week here in the church and she had promised to help.

'Of course, I didn't forget. That's why Arthur and I are here. We want the dead to look as tidy as the living.'

Diana doesn't quite like the tone of that but smiles to let it pass and pats Arthur on the head.

'So will you come in and help us? We can clean the pulpit for the service next week, too.'

They move to go in but Arthur hesitates on the porch.

'Isn't it a sin for a Catholic to go into a Protestant church?'

He whispers to her.

Elizabeth laughs.

'Not if you hold the hand of your Protestant godmother. The Pope himself allows that.'

'Are you sure.'

'You know I've been to Rome, don't you. I brought you back that picture of the Coliseum. So, you see, I am something of an expert on the rules of the Roman Catholic Church.'

The young couple push open the narrow door and walk on ahead, while the boy hangs back, half afraid of hell fire. Although he is twelve, he is glad of her hand to hold. Halfway up the aisle, he stops to read a tablet on the wall out loud and she stands by him. It is the memorial to her grandfather, the old Master, as Teresa calls him.

'Here we have no abiding city.'

'There,' Elizabeth tells him, 'Rome again, you see.'

At the altar, the young couple are muttering and looking over some papers. Diana hands Elizabeth a sheet of paper.

'We are thinking of asking Alan to read this for us. Do you think he will mind?'

She looks down.

'Let me not to the marriage of true minds admit impediment.'

She pushes the paper back into the young man's hands as quickly as she can.

'He will be delighted,' she says a little curtly, 'Arthur, let's go and finish off our work and let these two alone here.'

It is unfair of her but she cannot bear the happy egotism of their wedding plans.

Later, when John and Diana are gone, and Arthur is sent off with a wheelbarrow full of weeds to dump behind the vestry, she goes back into the church to lock up. She notices that she has left the watering can on a pew and strides up the empty church to retrieve it. Even on a warm day like today, the little church smells slightly of damp and the golden autumn light is opaque and dimmed as she walks up the central isle. She stands by the heavy pulpit, thinking, 'I don't think I've ever been alone in this church before in my life.'

On the ground she notices a sheet of paper and picks it up. The Shakespeare. She glances 'Love is not Love which alters when it alteration finds.'

All in a moment, as she was dreading, the vision of Charles and Sylvia standing before the altar comes to her with full wounding clarity. 'Of course,' she thinks, and isn't sure if she is saying this out loud, 'I always thought I would marry him' and the force of this hits her like a slap and she feels the strength drain from her limbs. A drumming in her ears begins and she wonders if she is going to fall. I thought I would marry him. And here. 'The star to every wandering bark.'

Behind her, just below the noise in her ears, humming like the planes over London, she thinks. She can hear footsteps coming up through the church. Arthur. No, she thinks, he shouldn't be here. She wants no witness to the harsh panting she is experiencing in her

Happy Autumn Fields Cork September 1947

chest, this final, awful collapse of her pride, the sobbing that she can feel breaking up the thin steel plate pressing against her chest. She clutches at the heavy wood of the pulpit, sinking into the solid bulk, and thinks, 'I am here and he is not. My Darling, My Darling, My Darling.' She can feel her shoulders begin to shake and her body buckles inwards and she grinds her forehead into the dark wood, feeling the skin beginning to rasp, welcoming the stinging feeling. As the first sob comes, made louder, somehow terrible by the high emptiness around her, Arthur creeps up to stand close by her side, by some miracle, wordlessly, without a sound or a question. All the tears she has denied suddenly move within her chest and she cries for the end of her wartime dream and the broken, unfinished, unfinishable novel lying on her desk, as broken as her dream of Charles in the moonlight of Regent's Park. Against her, as her sobs break out into full voice, she feels Arthur slowly, gently take her elbow, holding it delicately as if it were a bird's nest full of eggs, patting it awkwardly and she twists her body to burrow desperately into the solid indifference of the pulpit. Somehow her sobs seem to reach through to Arthur as well and she can feel him rest his forehead next to her into the pulpit and begin to sob gently, his arm now holding her elbow confidently, his grasp welcome and comforting. For what seems like an eternity, they stand there and then her breathing slowly steadies itself. All in a minute, Arthur takes a step away from her and peering around into her face, wet with tears, asks in a whisper.

'Mrs Cameron?'

'Yes,' she asks, her voice now calm, reassuring. 'What is it, Arthur?'

He says nothing but straightens up, moving imperceptibly away from her, to wait by her side as she lifts her hands to wipe her eyes dry, her breathing now calm. He goes over to collect the misplaced handbag.

'Will I bring this up to the house?'

The Last Day at Bowen's Court

'Do. You are a poppet.'

And she kisses him tenderly and wipes the stray tears from his beautiful face while he looks at her calm face, now reassured by the end of her awful, terrifying sobbing.

She walks back up to the house and taking Charles' letter, brings it up to her desk. Willing her heart to be still, she tears it open. One sheet. The familiar handwriting. She looks at the date. It is now two weeks old. Nothing could be as bad as that moment in the church and so she forces herself to read it.

'Dearest Elizabeth, Last night at dinner, the talk was all about you and the new novel and Nancy and Duff swearing that they would swoop down on you at Bowen's Court and force you to finish. They are convinced that you are the only one who can do justice to that time in London and I completely agreed with them. You MUST finish it, Elizabeth. Tonight, when I got back to this dismal flat, I had two strong whiskies and sat down to read your war stories again and now it is two in the morning and I order you to finish. Good God, they were right. You caught our siren years perfectly with your witch-like eye, (and you are a witch), our first moonlight walk, those drunken French soldiers, in the park and the Rider Haggard lines. Elizabeth, do pay attention to me, you must finish it, and you did promise me. I hold you to that promise. Love, as always Charles.'

Relief floods through her as she realises. No mention of Sylvia. Nothing but her. Her hand shaking with relief, she gets out her pen and writes back immediately. Her pen flows easily, as she tells him of Bowen's Court in the autumn, the gossip from London, Arthur's progress in school. She tells him that she will begin the novel again, and will send him updates as she writes.

She goes over to one of her suitcases and finds his framed photograph, the one from the mantelpiece in Clarence Terrace and puts it on the desk in front of her, just behind the typewriter. She knows that Teresa can see it when she comes in tomorrow with her morning tray but will say nothing, simply relieved to hear the sound of the typewriter morning after morning. Teresa probably thinks that the sight of Charles' face whenever she lifts her eyes from her work inspires her but it is not that. She needs to grow accustomed to it, wear away the sense of sudden emotion, and make his face as familiar as her own. He has become entangled around her heart like bindweed and so she must see his face day after day, that is the only way she will finish it. Picking up the manuscript, she starts to read and stays there until called away for dinner. Later, unusually for her, she returns to work in the early evening and finishes reading by midnight. She sleeps soundly and then gets up early, to start straight away.

As if to help her, the weather changes, autumn announcing itself in early September with a cooler feeling in the air, the light brighter, the sultry feeling gone, a hint of sharpness in the air. Outside her window, she can hear the cry of seagulls blown far inland and the occasional snap of a bough breaking far away in the forest. She wakes up early to start writing, and then after lunch, while she plans out her next pages, she listens to Alan's complaints and nods and tells him that she will finish the novel and with the American royalties, she will pay for a new bathroom and he looks relieved. The afternoons are bright and the September sunshine paler, with a touch of coolness and she walks the demesne for an hour or so to clear her head and plan her weekly letter to Charles.

One bright afternoon, at the stream by the old ruined mill, she hears a drumming in the air behind her, like the oncoming sounds of aircraft and wonders if she is hallucinating. But no. Three fully grown swans fly low over her head, thrilling her with their strength and their nearness and the drumming sound of their powerful flapping is like some kind of machine above her and she hurries home to write to Charles.

In one letter he tells her, 'In the midst of everything here in Paris, I find myself conjuring up the fields around Bowen's Court, like some kind of mirage of peace and of refuge and I envy you the full autumn glory right outside your window. Pick and eat some blackberries for me and then write and tell me, so that I can taste them myself. I was sitting at a very dull dinner last night and the powerful scent of roses from the garden outside suddenly transported me back to the porch at Bowen's Court and I day-dreamed my way back, imagining I was standing there, just arrived and your smile of welcome, the cigarette in your hand. Darling, it all came to me and I swore I would return.'

Often she returns in the afternoon and evening to wrestle with what she wants to say, and one day Teresa exclaims at a trace of blood on her forehead.

'You've cut your head open.'

Elizabeth looks in the mirror. There is a wound on her forehead, a patch of skin scrapped away. It is where she presses her knuckle into her forehead, in her concentration on the writing.

By her own reckoning, she is now writing seven hours a day or more, in her efforts to finish the chapter where her lovers Stella and Robert confront each other. One day she decided that she must put them in Charles' old attic flat in Whitehall, the one with the door out to the roof. The scene where she sends Robert out to die gives her a chilling but not unsatisfactory feeling, as if she is willing Charles' death or has already experienced his death. In a way, she supposes she has.

All around her life continues but she shuts it out, greedy for all the time she needs to finish the novel. Arthur asks her to look at his new school books but she keeps putting him off and Alan wakes up with a nasty stye on his eye one morning and demands that she bring him into Cork to the hospital. She phones Diana and John, just back from their honeymoon and they oblige and Teresa comes all the way up from

Happy Autumn Fields Cork September 1947

the kitchen to reproach her, tells her she should be giving Alan more attention but she ignores her, each day a precious time of writing, now extending it up to the evenings. In her letters to Charles, she keeps him informed of the progress of the novel, and of the doings of the house. He writes of his longing to see Farahy and his envy of her being there, in the midst of the autumn fields, while he must search out a place to live in Bonn. In her next letter, she broaches the subject of her love for him and tells him that from now on, she will be open about that in her letters. 'Love is a life and life does cry out to be lived.' He stops writing for a week or so and then another letter comes, full of news and still no mention of Sylvia.

Richard and Blanche arrive as promised early one morning at the end of October, with the autumn in full colour in Bowen's Court, and she hears their arrival from her room, the slamming of car doors, Alan's voice raised in happy vigour as he welcomes them. Just when she knows they are all there, she walks in, and hands over the finished manuscript triumphantly to Richard. His pleasure at seeing her is added to by the visible relief on his face. Alan's delight is evident too and he hurries to get champagne from Teresa and to get her to join in the celebrations. Elizabeth notices Blanche's face as she reads the dedication at the front of the novel and then composes herself to ignore it and comes over to kiss her and congratulate her.

Teresa comes in with the champagne and asks, 'So what are you calling this one?'

Before she can answer, Alan picks it up.

'*The Heat of the Day*, apparently. Very Shakespearean.'

They all raise their glasses, Richard clutching the manuscript to himself for dear life.

'To *The Heat of the Day*.'

Heat of the Day
London
1948

Sylvia sits drinking tea and thinks, 'Somewhere in London, my husband is meeting his mistress. She is bringing him a copy of the novel she wrote about their affair. I sip this tea and wonder about smashing the cup into the marble fireplace.' If mistress is the right word for Elizabeth. Lover? That makes her even angrier and yet she sits still.

It is their first week in London, their first holiday since they got married but, as Charles insists on saying, 'We won't call this a honeymoon, will we, Syl.' Now she sees why. She wonders if she should leave him. She contemplates taking the train back to their apartment in Paris this evening but, beyond that she hesitates. A return alone to Canada. Her marriage an open failure within the first year. A bleak prospect. She forces herself to sit still as the minutes tick by, tormented by the thought of Elizabeth with her husband.

Elizabeth has always been a concern for Sylvia. When Charles proposed to her last year, Sylvia wanted to ask about their affair but found that she couldn't quite frame the question. Elizabeth had been his mistress all during the war, or one of them at least, a famous writer and,

Heat of the Day London 1948

as Sylvia had always experienced her, a woman of formidable charm. If Elizabeth wanted you to like her, then it was hard to resist. Elizabeth had set out to befriend Sylvia when she was merely Charles' younger cousin over from Canada, and it had worked. Sylvia had come to like her. Indeed, more than like her. If she was honest with herself, she had become a little mesmerised by her. Besides, she was the first writer that Sylvia had ever known personally and so she devoured all of her novels and stories, entranced by their moments of heart stealing loneliness. Elizabeth's writing had burned into Sylvia's imagination. She knew that a woman who wrote like that had a soul of undoubted beauty and that worried her as she contemplated marrying Charles. Then, one day, just after Charles had asked her to marry him Sylvia answered the phone in his apartment and found herself at the receiving end of Elizabeth's rage. At first all she could hear was a strangulated sound, as Elizabeth struggled to speak. Then, all too soon her words became clear and Sylvia slammed down the phone to put an end to her stammering rage. She told Charles about the phone call and he frowned and told her it wouldn't happen again. After that, Elizabeth's name had disappeared from conversation.

When Charles proposed the London trip, Sylvia wondered about bringing up Elizabeth's name, but again found that she couldn't. For months now, it was as if Elizabeth had vanished. Sylvia began to breathe easily again. Until today happened.

It had been all so sudden. That morning at breakfast, Charles mentioned that he had some work to attend to and asked her to lunch. All week he had shown her his favourite places in London, Regent's Park in particular drawing him back again and again. Then, at lunchtime, when she returned to the hotel, a note was waiting for her on their bed. 'Change of plan. I'm meeting E at four. She has a copy of the new novel for me. I'll phone at 6. We will meet Alan and E somewhere for dinner, Charles.' Sylvia read it several times. E. No need to explain who E was. The new novel. The one about the war? She had read about it in the newspapers and Sylvia felt winded as it suddenly struck her. Was it about Elizabeth's affair with Charles? It must be!

She looks around and notices a book on top of a pile of Charles' papers. A new one. She picks it up. *The Demon Lover and Other Stories*. Elizabeth's, of course. Not one Sylvia has seen before. A folded piece of paper was left in the book where Charles had been reading. She opens at that page and sees it. 'Mysterious Kor', the last story in the volume.

Sylvia sits down on the bed and begins to read. A wartime story. A young couple, a soldier and his girl, wander around London at midnight, in blazing moonlight, with nowhere to make love, while her flatmate waits up for them at home, too innocent to realise that she is in the way. The night-time scene grips Sylvia, a deserted London now transformed into the ancient city of Kor, from one of her favourite childhood books, until she gets to the part of the story when the lovers return to the flat and find the naïve flatmate still waiting up for them, still in the way. As she reads, Sylvia begins to get angry. Callie, the innocent girl, her unsought out state, the braided hair, even the detail of her cretonne house coat. It was a portrait of Sylvia, from that first night during the war, when Charles had brought Elizabeth back to his flat and then slept on the couch. A simpleton child, caught between two lovers. In a rage, Sylvia flings the book at the wall and gets up and makes her way briskly downstairs, inquiring from the concierge about the nearest bookshop.

'The new Bowen! Sold out, Madam,' the nice young woman behind the counter tells her, looking pleased with herself. 'We shall have it back in stock next month. It's being reprinted. Would you care to order a copy? It's her best. A gripping love story.'

All afternoon, since she returned to the hotel empty-handed, Sylvia wonders what she should do. She knows that a stand needs to be made but exactly what? She thinks again about returning alone to Paris. 'A gripping love story.' The hunger to read it is like the fascination to prick one's thumb with a knife, anticipating the pain, the sting. She looks around at the others in the hotel drawing room and wonders if their lives are as puzzling as hers. Dinner for all four of them. Sylvia, Charles, Alan and Elizabeth. So cosy. How could they meet after that phone call last year?

She looks at her watch. Just after four. Sylvia picks up some coffee cake and begins to eat it, without appetite. Where are they? In a café, or a hotel lounge like this, or walking in the park or in bed? At this, she resolves to go upstairs and pack. She can leave Charles a note. Better still, no note. She has money and her passport, all of this could be arranged within the hour but still she sits there. It comes to her. Charles is the centre of Elizabeth's life. Now that they are married, she is somehow now Elizabeth's enemy. How can she win against her, all of that heady time together during the war, Elizabeth's diabolically clever writing? She must leave. It is her only defence. She finishes her tea and makes her way out of the lounge.

At reception she pauses.

'Can you order me a taxi for Paddington, please? I want to catch the seven o'clock boat train to Paris?'

She is nearly finished her packing when Charles phones.

'Syl, old girl, can you be here within the hour? I'm at Claridge's. Alan wants you to come too and join us for a cocktail.'

She murmurs something, looking at the book she had thrown at the wall, now lying looking wounded under the bedside table.

'What? I missed that. Look, can you hear me? Wear the new blue hat. Show your Parisian glamour!'

She hesitates and then he calls her name again.

'Syl. 6 p.m. in Claridges? Don't be late, old girl.'

She murmurs something non-committal, puts down the phone and looks out of the window. Her clothes are all packed but her hat is still on the dressing table. She picks it up and puts it on. She sees herself entering the hotel, in this smart blue hat and the gold band on her finger, wearing her nice dark cocktail dress from Paris. Something winds her again and she sits down on the bed and says out loud, trying out the words.

'Charles, the next time you meet Elizabeth, I will leave you. Is that clear?'

She looks at her watch, and, standing up, picks up the phone.

'I need to confirm my taxi, yes, 6 p.m.'

Charles is sitting at the bar when she enters, and an elderly man is standing talking to him, red faced, untidy-looking. As she draws nearer, she sees that it is Alan! It is less than two years since she dined in his flat in Clarence Terrace and it seems as if he has aged by a decade or more in the meantime. His left eye is inflamed and sore-looking and he has gained a great deal of weight. The whiskey glass in his hand shakes as he turns to greet her and she manages to keep the shock from her face.

'Sylvia, my dear, or Mrs Ritchie, as I must call you now. You look stunning, simply marvellous. Paris suits you, or marriage, or both.'

There is real warmth in his greeting and, on an impulse, she embraces him, surprised at her sudden rush of emotion towards him. He is reluctant to let her go, a tremor in his chest, travelling between them like a light touch of electric current and their foreheads bump gently together, a knock of recognition. Sylvia is glad of the embrace, afraid she might begin to weep. She turns to face Charles, who nods curtly. He is unusually bright-eyed and somewhat unlike himself, his customary calm assurance replaced by an energetic unease, his flushed face handsome and yet somehow bewildered. She gets the strongest feeling that he isn't really seeing her. He moves to kiss her cheek and she tilts her head away to look down. A book is sitting on the bar in front of him. Elizabeth's novel. She longs to take it up and look.

'Cocktail?' he asks and she nods, taking the seat that Alan has brought for her.

'Elizabeth is late.' Alan begins to fuss. 'Another interview for this book. I insisted she go back to the flat and rest.'

He fiddles with his cuffs, and then makes to stand up, a frown on his face.

'Maybe I should phone her up?'

Before Sylvia can stop him, Charles springs up from his chair, gently pushing Alan back into his seat.

'I'd completely forgotten. I promised to phone her up. Shan't be a moment.'

'Shouldn't Alan go?' She finds herself saying to his retreating back, but Charles is out of earshot, making his way quickly towards the hotel reception, leaving the book behind him on the counter. She looks down at it and Alan nods.

'There it is. Finally in print. You know, it cost her blood and tears to finish it. Literally. Nearly flattened her if the truth be told. Worth it in the end, I suppose?'

Alan talks on, as if to keep Sylvia from speaking, his eyes wandering restlessly around the crowded hotel bar.

'The dollars are rolling in from the US and all very welcome. Enough for a new bathroom in Bowen's Court. You must come over....'

He stops, realising what he is saying and then picks up the book and begins talking again.

'*The Heat of the Day*.'

'*The Heat of the Day*,' she repeats his words. '"Fear no more the heat

The Last Day at Bowen's Court

of the day/ and the winter's furious rages." Quite a title?'

Alan grimaces and then raises his finger to signal for another drink. She has barely touched her cocktail and now another joins it. Sylvia keeps looking at the book, hypnotised.

'The very quote. Never liked that speech myself. Had to learn it in school. "Golden lads and lassies must/ as chimney sweepers come to dust." Rubbing it in, rather.'

He laughs and then glances down, not really interested in her answer and she smiles as he starts to leaf through it, trying to look casual.

'Very striking,' she tells him, 'I tried to buy it today but it's sold out.'

Alan looks at her with some concern. He regards the book in his hands with a distinct air of mistrust.

'Haven't read it myself but everyone says it's marvellous, simply her best. Let me send you one.'

She smiles her thanks.

'In the meantime, I suppose Charles can lend you his copy, my dear.'

She shakes her head firmly, 'No. He is ruthless about his books. Nobody can borrow one. He was like that even as a teenager. May I?'

She reaches over to take it before he agrees, her patience now at an end. Reluctantly Alan hands it to her. She opens it and begins flicking. She comes to the dedication page.

'To Charles Ritchie.'

She flushes and snaps the book closed, slapping it back down on the bar, upsetting her cocktail. A splash of the vodka spatters the cover and begins to discolour the smart dusk jacket and she pokes a finger over to rub it off, muddying the ink on the cover. Unable to meet Alan's eyes, she struggles to keep her breath even. How dare Elizabeth! The chatter all around them in the bar covers up the silence that she is unable to break, knowing Alan to be watching her while she can feel heat building along her cheeks and her neck. The bar is beginning to clear, the first service of dinner being called and, after a few moments, she feels Alan's hand pat her lightly on the arm. Without looking up, she hears him murmur.

'I really don't mind, my dear. And you shouldn't, either. It's not important.'

Sylvia looks up him and he winces at the directness of her stare. After a moment, she begins. 'Elizabeth…She…How could she?' Alan crumples a little at her words and so she stops talking. He takes his time in replying, his face even more flushed, and it strikes her that he is more than a little annoyed at being forced into the open by her words.

'I don't mind for myself. Not at this point. I honestly don't. Bitha and I have been married for nearly thirty years now.'

He looks at her almost sternly. Bitha! Does Charles call her that, Sylvia wonders.

'After such a length of time, well, other considerations come into play.'

She nods, unwilling to listen but aware that she owes him some courtesy. He looks around, as if he longs to be in another part of the bar, chatting about the cricket with some chaps. The bar is almost clear now and he looks back at her, lowering his voice.

'I really shouldn't read it, if I were you. I shan't.'

He stops and then continues,

'It will only cause pain, in my opinion.'

Before she can stop herself, she bursts out.

'But…Alan. I'm leaving Charles. This…this is not to be tolerated.'

He smiles, not completely kindly and he speaks more crisply, as if wishing to impress her with hard facts, a well-intentioned teacher reprimanding a misguided student.

'So you say…Yet you sit here and wait for him. As I sit and wait for her. He married you. She has stayed with me because he didn't want her. That's all that matters. Not some book.'

He stops for a moment and then, his face becoming serious, his tone firmer.

'You don't know what it was like, last year, when she heard that you two were to be married. It almost unravelled her. Charles is her *idée fixe*. I hadn't quite realised how much. She looks ten years younger this week, like a newly released prisoner.'

He seems to be talking almost to himself and his air of authority keeps Sylvia silent. He spoke with the concentration of one facing one of the central fears of his life and Sylvia amends her tone.

'How can I live with her always looming in the shadows? She will be my *idée fixe* now?'

'Oh, I shouldn't worry. Charles is a decent sort, except when it comes to women, of course.'

Sylvia winces. Alan is entitled to this, she supposes, but it hurts.

'You know, during the war, when she was back in Ireland, waiting for his letters, it was my job to forward them on from London.'

He takes a long gulp of whiskey.

'I knew how she longed for them and once or twice I wondered about burning them or tearing them up. I couldn't. The thought of her pain stopped me. You can't fight that, can you?'

Alan turns to see Charles returning, his brow dark. He looks at them both with ill-concealed bad temper, as if they are somehow the offending parties and tells them, in a tone that will not brook questioning.

'Elizabeth has a headache. We are to eat without her. You finished, Syl? The table is ready.'

Heat of the Day London 1948

He picks up the book and puts it into the inside pocket of his suit, and all through the meal, it rests there, like a gangster's gun. That night, in the hotel room, when he opens the door, the first thing he sees is the packed suitcase on the bed. He turns to face her.

'Packing? Why?'

Put like that, she feels her determination falter.

'I'm going back to Paris, Charles. First thing in the morning.'

She sounds unconvincing, even to herself.

He shakes his head, as if to clear it and again looks annoyed with her.

'Is this to do with Elizabeth?'

'Yes. It is. You know how she spoke to me on the phone last year. How can you meet her after that?'

The powerlessness of her situation makes her sink down on the bed. Charles kneels beside her and takes one of her hands. She draws it away and stares down at the floor, needing to keep her concentration.

'Syl, you knew about Elizabeth before we got married.'

There is something in his tone that she liked, despite hating what he was saying. She reminds herself that Charles has always been honest with her. She stays quiet while he continues.

'But, I married you and not her. If you can bear that in mind, then I…well I would ask you to stay. Can you forget what she said? She was, well, more than a little unsteady.'

Something still nags her and she finally finds the words she was looking for.

'Charles, she has to meet me and be civil. I am your wife and she must treat me as such.'

He considers all she says and then nods.

'That's fair. I'll make sure that happens.'

He picks up the suitcase, hands it to her and stands watching as she begins to unpack. He retrieves the torn book from the floor and she says nothing.

Over the next few days, late at night, Sylvia slips out of bed to read Elizabeth's novel. He keeps it in his briefcase amongst his diplomatic papers, taking it away with him every morning when he goes out to the office. She imagines him reading it at his desk, drinking in every word, reliving those siren years and perhaps dreading what Elizabeth might do to him in her novel. Is this her revenge? As night, while he sleeps, Sylvia reads the same chapters, shadowing him, equally curious to know what Elizabeth made of him and of herself, with Alan's words echoing in the ears. 'Shouldn't read it. I won't.'

She is careful not to disturb anything as she lifts the novel out of his briefcase and takes it with her into the bathroom. She knows that once he falls asleep, nothing will wake him until the morning alarm and so she settles herself into the bath to start her reading, her dressing gown keeping her warm, the tap sometimes dripping, Charles snoring in the other room. Her first night reading was almost her last, with her anger at the written dedication she reads first, in Elizabeth's handwriting and it moves her to angry tears. The few lines in ink, beautifully crafted…'My Darling, My Darling, My Darling, we have walked a country together.'

But soon she steels herself to read on and is glad that she does. With her limited time to read, she soon learns to skip certain sections, anything with the young girl Louie and she waits impatiently to meet the lover Robert. And Stella fascinates her, the two lovers, clearly Elizabeth and Charles. Despite herself, Sylvia comes to love the novel, and wonders what Charles feels each morning as he reads his own life turned into fiction, in the intervals when he isn't attending to his letters or phoning his office in Paris. Is he flattered, or exhilarated?

All that week, late into the night, Sylvia reads quickly, in case that

Heat of the Day London 1948

Charles for once, wakes up and comes looking for her. Each chapter is marked with her husband's presence, his face, his hands, all the evidence of their wartime love affair, the reading pains her and leaves her feeling raw and wounded. All the next day as she walks or shops or sits at lunch with Charles, listening to his account of office politics, she thinks, does he see himself as Elizabeth sees him? As she reads, what shocks Sylvia most is that Charles has brought her to the very places of his love affair with Elizabeth, the Rose Garden, now and the places that Stella and Robert inhabit? For the rest of the week, she manages to make her excuses when Charles suggests that they visit Regent's Park but she wonders if he goes there alone.

The weekend is approaching fast and they have been invited to visit in the country for a few days when Charles phones her from the office on the Friday. He sounds uncomfortable.

'Syl, can you meet me at the V and A at three today? Alan just phoned, we are invited to tea, and they have a borrowed place just around the corner?'

They stand outside the white terrace in South Kensington, the bell ringing in the hall, not looking at each other. Sylvia thinks of the novel and of the intensity with which she is swept up by Elizabeth's writing and thinks, 'I don't stand a chance against her. I shouldn't be here.' Before she can pursue this thought, the door opens and Alan is standing there, his hands outstretched.

'Short on staff today, I'm afraid, I'm on door duty. Come on up, tea's ready.'

They go up to the first floor, into a room with a cosy fire and tea already on the low table. No Elizabeth. Alan looks at Sylvia.

'Can you be mother?'

They sit and Sylvia pours tea and the two men talk for a while, while Sylvia sits and wonders if Elizabeth has backed out of this.

The double doors slide open and Elizabeth stands there. Sylvia hasn't seen her for two years. Although pale and strained looking, she hasn't seen her looking better, a little thinner, with the full light of the early evening sun behind her.

The men fall silent and Sylvia, remembering the dedication, suppresses a polite urge to stand up and shake her hand. For what seems an eternity, Elizabeth stands there looking directly at Sylvia. This goes on until Charles says once, sharply 'Elizabeth'. And she looks as if she is finally preparing to speak. Her jaw works and her face becomes a little flushed but no words come out and Sylvia realises that her words are failing her. She begins to stutter, 's…s…s…' but the agony of strangulation keeps her from finishing her word. Sylvia wants this to stop, when she realises it is her own name that Elizabeth is struggling with. This charming English drawing room, the sunlight behind her, the two men watching in a kind of horror, all of these things seem only to exist to contain these prolonged, agonised moments. Sylvia watches Elizabeth's eyes, glittering like a startled horse, as she struggles to say her name and moisture leaks out of the side of her mouth. The moment, and it only can have been a moment although it seems to have been an eternity, ends when Alan puts down his cup with a clatter. The noise breaks the deadlock in the room and Elizabeth ceases her agonised struggles to speak. Alan walks over to his wife, saying, 'Enough now. Come along, Bitha.' At this point Elizabeth gazes helplessly at her husband who takes her by the shoulders and pushes her back into the room, screening her from Sylvia's and Charles' horrified gaze with his broad shoulders. The double doors close with a thud. A murmur of voices reach them, cut off from the evening sunlight. Stranded in a suddenly darkened room, Sylvia looks at Charles, standing there with a helpless look in his face that mirrors Elizabeth's. The room has become tainted

Heat of the Day London 1948

for Sylvia, as if she has just stood by and watched violence or even murder being committed without raising a finger. She needs to leave, to get away from this overheated room and rapidly picks up her hat and coat. When she sees Charles looking longingly at the closed double doors, she takes him firmly by the arm.

'We need to leave now, Charles.'

He shakes off her arm roughly but she takes it again without hesitation and he finally submits to being led away.

They leave for the country the next day and late that evening, after dinner and during bridge, Sylvia sees her chance. She has almost finished reading Elizabeth's novel, pleading a headache that afternoon while Charles goes out for golf, she took the novel from his briefcase and made her way upstairs. Lying in her bedroom with the door locked against Charles' return, she reads up to the point of confrontation between the two lovers when Stella, or Elizabeth, as Sylvia thinks of her, now confronts Robert with his treachery. 'For Germany, read me,' Sylvia thinks grimly. Afternoon tea and the sounds of the returning walkers interrupts her reading and she hurries to put the book back in Charles' briefcase. All through dinner, she wonders about finishing the novel, impatient to read to the end, and so when Charles excuses himself, with some letters to write, to her delight, Sylvia sees that he has left the novel on the ground near his seat, unnoticed by the others. Picking it up unobserved, she takes the book away with her into her host's Library, a large and somewhat neglected room, and, keeping an eye out for Charles, she finishes it. The scene of Robert's fall from the roof shocks her, and makes her wonder, does Elizabeth want him dead? Is my marriage death to her?

Swiftly, before she can change her mind, she walks over to a tall bookcase at the back of the Library, behind a sofa, and pushes the sofa to one side. Stooping down, she notices some large volumes. Old

The Last Day at Bowen's Court

Victorian bound copies of *Punch*, dusty and clearly neglected. Pulling one out, she jams Elizabeth's novel in the space behind it. Replacing the large tome, she is pleased to see that it fits back in seamlessly and then, pushing the sofa back into place, she makes her way to bed where Charles is already sleeping.

The next day Charles spends some time looking around the lounge, without telling Sylvia why? Later, in the hallway, she hears him ask the host about the maid, who is summoned and who bristles and feels as if she is being accused of something. As she listens, she wishes she could phone Alan and tell him what she has done but she knows that she will never see him again. The thought of Elizabeth's novel firmly wedged behind those old copies of *Punch* cheers her up on the train back to Paris, sitting quietly by Charles' side.

The Churchyard in Farahy Cork August 1952

It comes as a shock to Charles, on the day of Alan's funeral that Elizabeth's family close ranks on him, united in their attempts to keep him away from her. When she finally turns around and sees him in the graveyard, she looks at him, beseeching him to save her from all of this but she is surrounded by family. Arriving late, he is trapped at the back of the church but, later in the churchyard, Charles makes several attempts, but each time, an aunt or a cousin intercepts him. Laying a black gloved hand on his arm, one or other begins to chat and lead him as far away from her as possible. In the end, he gives up and stays at the back of the crowd, wondering at the profound change in attitude by her family. He lights a cigarette and stands there in the clear light of that bright August morning in North Cork, trying to remain calm. Looking around, he thinks, 'This is the kind of light I dream about whenever I think about Elizabeth's home in Ireland and the fields around her house.' He tells himself that if he had known that this would be happening, he wouldn't have travelled all this way to be at Alan's funeral. After all, her family have known all about him for many years, even her formidable Aunt Myra would refer to him in letters to Elizabeth as 'my darling Charles'. When Alan was alive, Charles' status as her lover had been accepted and even welcomed and he had been made one of the family on his visits to Dublin and here in Farahy, careful to visit always in Alan's absence. Now, with Alan unexpectedly dead, there is a distinct change in temperature and Charles stands at the edge of the crowd, shut out, firmly but politely. He smiles at one or two neighbours standing near him, remembering them from his previous trips. In a fit of anger, he contemplates driving back to Cork without another word, leaving it all behind, his hurried trip here a failure. Sylvia had warned him that he would not be wanted here but he hung up the phone on her. But he thinks of Elizabeth's plea for him to come and be with her at the funeral and he finds that he cannot leave.

Elizabeth's call had come to him in Bonn, early in the morning three days previously, just as he was leaving for his office, catching him unawares.

'Charles? Can you speak?'

Her voice sounded hushed and more than a little frightened. Sylvia was in Canada tending to her mother and this leaves him free to speak but he wonders at this unexpected call.

'Yes, of course. Just on the way to the office but I do have a few minutes. What is it? You sound a little strange.'

There is a pause while she struggles with her words.

'I...I'm afraid it's Alan...I found him this morning.'

Just at that moment, with her usual terrible timing, his German housekeeper pushes her noisy vacuum through the open door, drowning out Elizabeth's voice. He drops the phone, waving at Greta to leave, and then runs over to kick the door closed behind her, ensuring she stays out. She will sulk for hours, Charles thinks, but he doesn't care.

The Churchyard in Farahy Cork August 1952

He picks up the phone again, half hoping that Elizabeth had been cut off by this.

'I'm sorry, Bitha, that idiotic Greta disturbed me. She has a gift for appearing exactly when she isn't wanted.'

He is playing for time. Alan dead. This is unwelcome news.

'He looks very peaceful,' Elizabeth continued, the same calm tone, with an undercurrent of fear, as if he had not spoken. 'We haven't moved him yet. It must have happened during the night.'

'What happened?'

Her voice sounds young and vulnerable and Charles curses his lateness in leaving for work.

'His heart, I suppose. I went in at eight and I knew there was something wrong. He was lying on his back. He could never bear to lie on his back....'

She pauses and Charles wishes he could stop her. He feels as if he has stumbled into Alan's bedroom and this vision image of Alan lying dead on his bed won't leave him.

'I called Teresa and we got the doctor out from Mallow but it was too late. He had slipped away.'

He listens in silence and then she calls his name again.

'Charles? Are you there?'

'Yes.'

Charles looks at the picture of his wife on his desk. What will Sylvia think when she hears? She had always liked Alan. So did Charles, when he comes to think of it.

'I am so sorry, my dear, so sorry, Elizabeth. I always liked Alan, you know,' he says, his mind racing.

'And so you did,' Elizabeth murmurs down the phone, the first trace of tears in her voice. 'And I feel so bad for all those letters I wrote to you complaining about him. He's been so difficult for the last few months, I simply had to tell someone.'

Elizabeth's letters are kept in his office in work, out of Sylvia's way and the recent ones lament Alan's morning drinking, his quarrels with the neighbours, her weariness with his endless complaints about Bowen's Court. Charles makes a note to tear them up.

The remorse in her voice prompts him to ask.

'How can I help?'

'Can you come over, Charles? I don't think I can get through this without you, I really don't.'

'Of course,' he answers before he can think properly. He was dreading that and the relief in her voice is clear and makes him feel even worse.

'That would be wonderful. I'd better go now, the house is beginning to fill up. The countryside is converging on us. The service is on Friday. Not much time but that's how funerals happen in Ireland.'

He puts down the phone and then picks it up again to call his secretary and tell her to book him on the afternoon train to Paris. It is only when he stops in London for a night to wait for the boat train that he summons up the resolve to phone Sylvia. She is surprised to hear from him, their weekly call arranged for Saturday night. He gets straight to the point.

'Alan has died.'

'I'm very sorry to hear that. He was always very kind to me.'

She sounds genuinely concerned, if a little wary.

'Will you put my name on some flowers and send them to Cork?'

'I can bring some. I'm travelling there now. I'm in London and I'll be in Cork just in time for the funeral tomorrow.'

Silence and then she raps out.

'Is that…necessary? You should have discussed this with me first. And, apart from anything else, will you be wanted there?'

The Churchyard in Farahy Cork August 1952

'I think so,' Charles shoots back. 'He's been a friend of mine for the last ten years.'

Sylvia laughs. It is an unpleasant laugh and Charles has come to dislike it. There is a dry tone to it that irritates him.

'Hardly that. Charles, it is not your place to be there. Besides she has all of her family and her friends there with her. All those terrifying aunts. They won't want to see you on display, believe me, however much she does.'

At that, he hangs up and then tries to phone her back but the phone rings out and nobody answers. He can see Sylvia standing there, a grim look on her face, her mother calling querulously from upstairs for someone to answer that phone.

In London, he finds a copy of a newspaper with details of Alan's funeral. He needs to take the night boat to Cork to get there in time. In Cork, arriving in the luminous half-light of an August dawn, he breakfasts and bathes in a hotel and then drives himself out to Farahy, the glorious weather lighting the harvested fields on each side of the road and he longs to pull over and lie down in the sunlight and sleep in the embrace of these impossibly golden worlds. Hedge roses brush against the open window of the car as he pulls in.

Arriving just as Alan's coffin is being brought into the crowded churchyard, he hurries in with the tail end of the crowd through the narrow porch. As he comes in, one or two local people nod to him, recognising him from his previous visits and he surveys the church. The seats are full and the sides crammed with men in dark coats, standing uncomfortably pressed up against the wall. He wonders about making his way up to the top of the church, where he can see Elizabeth standing with her back to the congregation, her arm around her elderly housekeeper Teresa, but he decides to remain where he is and, with some difficulty, finds a place to stand at the back of the church.

The clergyman enters to begin the service, all present standing with an uprising swish. As the murmur of prayers start, Charles begins to find the heat of the church and the unpleasant smell of damp and of the many people crammed in together unsettling. For a moment he finds himself swaying a little on his feet, the long journey now taking effect and he longs for his slim pocket-size whiskey flask, left behind in Bonn. He tries to stay awake by looking around at the memorials on the walls of the small church while the clergyman intones the endless prayers of consolation and one male cousin after another stands up to read. Charles cannot recall if he has been here before. Surely Elizabeth had shown him the church on one of his visits? The place is dank, the whitewashed walls speckled with damp, an unwashed feeling in the air. Nearby, he can see a white marble plaque. A memorial to Robert and Elizabeth Bowen, her grandparents to judge by the dates. He reads the inscription. 'Here we have no abiding city, for we wait for the city to come.' A memory comes back to him, of a graveyard in Hythe, but what it means he cannot recall. Did he read about it in one of her books or did she tell him? As the prayers come to an end, the clergyman motions them to sit. Charles wonders about Alan's faith. Did he believe in the city to come? Somehow he doubts it. He knows that Elizabeth has no such faith and wonders what is sustaining her at the moment.

He peers forward, cursing his fogged up glasses to watch Elizabeth, in black but unveiled, sitting on the front row next to the coffin, her arm linked by her Aunt Myra on one side. On her other side, her housekeeper Teresa sits. She turns and looks down the aisle. Teresa settles down as the young clergyman, fleshy and with a booming voice, begins his homily about the dead man. It is soon clear that the young man has never actually met Alan but he does his best, making the most of his war record, and mentioning his injuries.

The Churchyard in Farahy Cork August 1952

Charles had never known that Alan had been injured in the Great War and his sight compromised. The clergyman talks on for a while and then slowing down, clearly coming to the point, emphasises his words with even greater meaning, and the congregation respond with a ripple of movement, anticipating a release from this endless homily.

'Alan was much loved here in Farahy where he retired with his wife Elizabeth to devote himself to the maintenance of the house, now nearing its two hundredth anniversary, and also to devote himself to his wife's distinguished writing career, a source of true pride to him. And today we know that his own faith is fulfilled by his return to the Lord, his belief in family, in country and in his duties to those around him sustain him and bring him to his just reward. As Alan knew of this life, we wait for the city to come. Today Alan has found that city and we rejoice on his behalf.'

'Do we?' thought Charles, 'I can't imagine Alan is pleased to be gone, however difficult he found life for the last few months.'

Then they all stand to sing 'Now the Day is Over' and Charles hears some sobs around him but, as far as he can see, Elizabeth stands calmly, singing, her arm tightly around Teresa. As they sing, Charles recalls Elizabeth's letters of the past few months, her finding Alan asleep on the sofa in the Library early one morning, clearly not having been to bed at all, an empty whiskey flask beside him and his anger on being woken and pushed upstairs to bed with Teresa's help, the scene in the tax office in Cork where Alan swore at a young civil servant who told him the old days of empire were over and she would call the Gardaí. It took all of Elizabeth's charm to soothe the young woman in the tax office and now today, in the crowded churchyard, all of this has been elided. Only the best of the man is remembered and Charles wonders if it's hypocrisy or simple human kindness? Charles is unsure. Dubious kindness probably, face saving at its best?

The Last Day at Bowen's Court

At last, the clergyman blesses them for a final time, signalling that the service has come to an end and they all stand while the undertakers in neat black make their way silently to the front and surround the coffin, as if there to arrest Alan, waiting respectfully for Elizabeth to rise and lead the procession. There seems to be some delay with Teresa, and finally Elizabeth takes her by the arm and they turn and begin to walk towards the door, Aunt Myra and Angela leading the procession of the family behind them while the congregation stand in respectful silence. Now, Charles thinks, now she will see me. But, her head bowed, her arm in Teresa's, her eyes fixed firmly on Alan's coffin in front of her, she walks past him, almost near enough for her to touch her and it gives him a chilling feeling not to be seen by her.

The church slowly empties and Charles is one of the last to emerge into the gentle sunlight. Alan's coffin has now been placed on a plinth in front of the church door where another clergyman has joined the vicar and they begin their prayers right out in the open. The graveyard is full, now, with many more people than can have been in the tiny church. Charles remembers Elizabeth telling him that when her father died, they held the service for him in the graveyard, out of respect for the many Catholic neighbours. These must be the good neighbours of Farahy, Kildorrery and beyond as far as Fermoy and Mallow and this new clergyman the local parish priest. It is a warm day, the dew still on the older Bowen graves near Charles' feet, and the air is clean and fragrant, welcome to him after his overnight travel. The fresh breeze blows from the direction of the farmland surrounding them, bringing the delicious scent of freshly mown hay. Through the hedge, Charles catches a glimpse of the fields. Golden stubble after the harvest, birds on the prowl over the opened ground, crying to each other in glee. The prayers end and then the coffin is brought over to the freshly dug grave, silence in the churchyard as the priest and the vicar join forces

The Churchyard in Farahy Cork August 1952

to sprinkle the coffin with water, the only sound a kind of distressed murmur from Teresa. Charles has a clear view of Elizabeth as she looks down at the coffin, and he admires her composure, her dark clothes, her eyes downcast, a single silver ornament on her coat. A present from Alan, he recalls, marking their twenty-fifth wedding anniversary. There is an imperceptive tightening of the crowd around her as Alan's coffin is lowered into the grave with the murmur of prayers from the clergyman. Charles finds himself pushed right to the back of the crowd, unable to see more than Elizabeth's back, in deep black, her head bent low, with her aunt's arm around her neck, holding on to her firmly.

Pale but collected and looking very handsome in black, she moves to place her wreath on Alan's coffin as it is lowered down, her Aunt Myra gripping her tightly in case she thinks about joining Alan. Something about the way she is standing tells Charles that Aunt Myra is worrying needlessly. He watches Elizabeth with admiration and a surprising tenderness as she turns around and begins shaking hands with all of those who had come to the service now lining up to pay their respects to her. He thinks, how rare it is for him to stand and watch her and she is admirable in her composure. Charles makes his move to join her, but her cousin Angela steps in his way, to throw her arms around him and hug him. When she melts away, wordless, Charles can still see Aunt Myra keep a firm hold on her and a circle of female cousins encircle Elizabeth as she greets the large crowd and chats with each person, her voice audible to Charles on the edge of the crowd, confident and distinct, with an occasional light ring of laughter. The tension of the funeral is broken by that laughter. Around him people begin to chat to neighbours, to light cigarettes and gradually the sound of chatter fills the small graveyard.

And then, all in a moment, Charles is horrified to be suddenly at the centre of attention. Teresa, who has wandered away from Elizabeth, spots him and, pushing her way through the crowd around the grave, throws herself into his arms with a great cry. Embarrassed and at the same time distressed for her, he tries to console her as she starts to sob, her grey head pressed against his chest, but worse follows as she starts to gabble at him, to be heard by all of those around her.

'There you are, Alan. I was looking for you everywhere. Go over to her now. Look at her, she needs you and we are burying her father today.'

Charles is dumbfounded while the old woman looks up at him with impatience and puzzlement,

'Why are you standing over here?'

In the silence that follows, Charles looks around to find Elizabeth staring directly over at him from the graveside, her pale face showing the first flush of colour. By the expression in her eyes, Charles can see that she is in shock, but nevertheless her wits are working as she watches Teresa cling to him. She excuses herself from a clergyman who has her hand trapped in his and makes her way quickly through the crowd towards them, holding out her arms to encircle Teresa. In one movement, she prises Charles from Teresa's demented grasp.

'Teresa, darling, can you come with me? I have your lovely wreath from home, the roses from the front porch and it's time to put them on Alan's…' she starts to stammer… 'To leave them here for Alan.'

Teresa looks confused, and points up to Charles, her hand grasping his lapel.

'Sure, isn't Alan right here?'

And she peers up at Charles, a look of doubt crossing her face.

Elizabeth looks over at Charles, to hush him and then turns to Teresa, speaking softly, gently but firmly.

'No, my darling. This is Charles. Charles is here to carry the wreath with you, Teresa. He has travelled all the way from Germany to say goodbye to Alan. Let's go over and collect the wreath for him now.'

Elizabeth nods knowingly at Charles, who begins to prize Teresa's

The Churchyard in Farahy Cork August 1952

fingers from his sleeve, and looking into the old woman's eyes, says as clearly as she can.

'Teresa, this is Alan's funeral. We found him on Wednesday in his bed, the poor dear. Remember? Well, now, it's time to say goodbye to him. And to give him our best love. Come now.'

A sob escapes from Elizabeth but her voice remains firm. Elizabeth draws Teresa away and, as if from nowhere, Aunt Myra takes Charles' arm and gives him a kiss.

'My dear Charles, when did you arrive? You are a dear to come here just for a few hours?'

Unwilling to talk to her now, he turns back to watch Elizabeth leading Teresa out of the graveyard and into a waiting car, the old woman sobbing gently, Elizabeth patting her shoulder, both of them murmuring. As soon as the car pulls off, Aunt Myra is gone too, disappearing into the crowds leaving the churchyard.

Unwilling to be left alone with Alan's open grave, he leaves and wonders about walking up to the house, the morning air clearing his head, the birds scattering ahead of him and he is reminded again of how much he loves these fields, especially in autumn. He didn't think he would be seeing them so soon and in these circumstances. He wanders out of the church and makes his way down to his rented car. As he turns the corner, a young man calls after him and hurries to catch up with him, neatly dressed in a dark suit and his hair smooth. He stops.

'Mr Ritchie?'

Charles peers at the young man.

'Yes?'

The young man blushes.

'It's me. Arthur.'

'Arthur. Good God. You are a grown man now. I can't believe it.'

They shake hands warmly. It seems like yesterday since he had walked with this boy up the avenue, to collect eggs and now he is as tall as himself, with fashionably brylcreemed dark hair. Yet Charles can still see the boy in this newly grown man.

'It's wonderful to see you, Arthur. How is life in Dublin treating you?'

Charles recalled Elizabeth telling him that Arthur was studying to be a doctor, with Alan's active encouragement and the young man blushes with pleasure at his recollection. Well, at least this is one moment when being a diplomat has its advantages.

'Mrs Cameron wants me to bring you up to the house. There's a room ready.'

Charles hesitates. He remembers the family and the trick they had of getting between him and Elizabeth.

'Are you sure? I can get a hotel room in Mallow.'

'That's what Mrs Cameron has arranged. I can drive your car up.'

Arthur smiles at him. At least he seems glad to see him.

'Now. No arguing. I'm to bring you up now or else I'm in big trouble.'

In the car, Charles asks about Teresa. A dark look crosses Arthur's young brow.

'Mrs Cameron is after calling for the doctor in Fermoy again. Teresa is lying down now but I don't know what'll happen to her. Do you know, when I called down to the kitchen this morning with the crates of stout for the wake, she didn't know who I was, and I up in that kitchen for years. Told me to be about my business.'

Arthur looks genuinely upset, the years of affection apparently wiped out in the old woman's mind, the shock of Alan's death unhinging her.

'To be honest, it couldn't come at a worse time. The mother was only saying to me before the funeral mass, Mrs Cameron will be lost without Mr Cameron. He did everything with the banks and all that.

The Churchyard in Farahy Cork August 1952

She's like a child when it comes to serious business.'

Charles listens without comment, aware that Arthur's shrewd old mother will already have told him of speculations around his own future role here.

'Now here we are. And the place is crawling with people. I better get back in the kitchen and start cutting more sandwiches.'

Charles parks his hired car around the back of the house, next to the walled garden and stands smoking for a few minutes, reluctant to be part of the chattering crowd inside. It is a warm day and all the windows are open and laughter and the clink of glasses fill the air. He wonders if this will be the last great gathering in Bowen's Court. He looks at the house, its unwieldy bulk, its stone glittering lightly in the sun and remembers his first sight of the house and how disappointed he had been when he saw it. Now, he has come to love it with a great deal of passion, thinking of the rooms, and the fields around at unbidden moments in his travels. Was this the end or a new beginning? He throws his cigarette away and braces himself to enter the thronged house. And still he hesitates. From an open window, he hears two men chatting.

'Have some more of this sherry, Father, Alan was very proud of it, God be good to him.'

A clink of glasses.

'I wonder if this place will last. She will find it a huge burden.'

Charles hurries into the house, unwilling to listen to any more, and finds himself a much needed whiskey. He is put on duty with the drinks by Aunt Myra who runs the whole operation with consummate skill and Elizabeth finds herself being brought away again and again for confidential chats by neighbours, or to sign for telegrams or wreaths that keep arriving until well into the night. There is something theatrical about the day as it unfolds. The occupants of the house, Charles now included, actors in the ongoing drama of Alan's wake, the constant stream of visitors driving up to the front porch, Elizabeth standing on the open door of the Library to greet them and pass them on for tea to Angela or to Charles for something stronger. Arthur ferries sandwiches up from the kitchen until he looks blue with tiredness but insists on continuing. By evening Elizabeth is hoarse from the constant talking but refuses to go and lie down, despite Aunt Myra prodding at Charles to persuade her. Elizabeth's aunt make the best of it and works him unmercifully. Now in her late seventies, she has the stamina of a woman half her age and keeps up a running commentary.

'The curate from Fermoy. RC, not ours. Father O'Connor or Connell, drat it. Can never remember, tiresome little man.'

She beams her full smile.

'Father, you are so kind. My niece will be pleased to see you. Some tea perhaps or something stronger. Mr Ritchie will see to you. A glass of Alan's whiskey is my recommendation.'

At eight, Charles brings Elizabeth a stiff drink and some food. She takes it gratefully.

'Bitha,' he whispers. 'You really should lie down for a while. The doctor gave me these. They should help.'

He slips her a packet of sleeping tablets. She shakes her head, dark circles under her eyes, her face pale.

'Darling, imagine what the Bowen ghosts would make of me if I deserted my post. Honestly, I'm fine.'

Exhausted, Charles slips away to bed, a half bottle of whiskey to help him sleep and wonders if he should try and phone Sylvia. Over a late breakfast the next morning, with no sign of Elizabeth, Aunt Myra monopolises him, telling him unending tales of family houses sold up, the impossibility of paying rates, the young people leaving the country.

'I don't know why Alan spent so much time getting that scholarship for young Arthur, he will have to go and work in Canada as soon as he is qualified, there's no work in this country.'

'Canada! Would that be so bad?'

Aunt Myra colours a little at Charles' smile.

'Not that Canada isn't a wonderful country. Well, indeed, are you not a shining example.'

Charles takes advantage of her momentary embarrassment to rout her further.

'And we are moving back next month, you know. I've been given a new job in Ottawa. Sylvia is very pleased, she can be near her mother, who is very poorly.'

Aunt Myra looks at him most peculiarly, as if this unexpected mention of his wife of five years is somehow unsavoury.

Somewhat to her relief, the door opens and Elizabeth enters. Charles had found it impossible to speak to her last night, what with all the visitors and also the doctor attending to Teresa. He had taken his whiskey bottle to bed early. And it strikes him that she looks exhausted.

'Well?' Aunt Myra looks at her inquiringly.

'The doctor has just now taken her into Cork, for tests. In his own car. She didn't want to go. You don't know what lies I had to tell her to get her into the car.'

She rubs her eyes, a shudder rippling down her shoulders. Aunt Myra stands up and kisses her.

'You are doing your best, Bitha. Always remember that. It is for Teresa's own sake.'

Elizabeth turns to Charles and smiles, as if to ask for forgiveness for bothering him with all of this. He looks at her reassuringly, and nods to ask.

'What will happen to her? She seemed very confused yesterday.

Maybe it was the shock of losing Alan? It may pass.'

She shakes her head sadly.

'The doctor thinks not. There were signs of this all summer, not just the funeral, Alan had noticed too... She needs permanent care. Apparently this place in the city might suit? The good nuns there have a place for her.'

She looks embarrassed as she mentions this. Charles can only imagine Teresa's bewilderment at being taken away from Bowen's Court. He remembered her telling him that she came there as a girl of seventeen, in Elizabeth's grandfather's time, the old master as she called him. He had gone mad, too, like her father. He wondered how Elizabeth was bearing up but she looked calm enough to him.

'I had to smuggle a small case with some of her clothes into the boot of the car. He wants me to bring more in later.'

Elizabeth takes the coffee he hands her and throws him a look of gratitude. Her aunt watches and says nothing, sensing a crisis and wisely keeping quiet.

'I suppose I really should keep her here, and get a nurse in for the mornings or someone to help but I'm due to be in the US next month, the money has already been paid and then there is the Rome book to do.'

Neither Charles nor Aunt Myra says anything. Elizabeth is clearly talking to herself, trying to convince herself that she is doing the right thing. Her aunt nods and pats her hand but says nothing and it occurs to Charles that her aunt may not approve of Teresa being sent off to a home in Cork but is unwilling to say anything. Charles suddenly stands up.

'Elizabeth, I'm so sorry but I really need to phone my office.'

She looks a little startled but nods.

'Of course, in the Library. Just help yourself.'

The Churchyard in Farahy Cork August 1952

He sits at her desk and waits for the operator to connect him. All around him, bank books and legal documents sit in neat piles. Already he can see that Elizabeth has started writing notes. She will be weighed down with all of this and looks tired already. He imagines her working there, trying to makes sense of it all, all her plucky strength needed. The phone rings and he hears Sylvia answering.

'It's me. Please don't hang up.'

She sighs.

'I suppose you went after all.'

'Yes, I'm there now. Look, I don't want to talk about that. About that offer in Ottawa?'

'Yes.'

She sounds cautiously interested.

'What if I say yes?'

'But you don't want to leave Europe. That's what you said. You said it would be a living death to come home.'

His wife has an excellent memory. She would have made a good novelist but he isn't inclined to tell her that at the moment.

'I know. But this is a promotion and they are talking about a move on to Washington in two years. Full Ambassador to the UN.'

'But you were dreading Ottawa.'

'With your mother ill, it would suit…'

Sylvia interrupts him.

'Don't make my mother part of the decision. Let's be honest. You've changed your mind. You want to leave Europe and get away from her. That's fine by me but I did warn you not to go to the funeral.'

The door opens quietly and Elizabeth walks in, holding up her hand apologetically. He waves her in.

'Look, I have to go now, I'll phone you when I get back to Bonn on Tuesday morning then? My office sent the booking for the Paris train on to my London address, the usual hotel. You can get me there tomorrow night?'

Sylvia laughs down the phone.

'O.K., you are clearing out. That's all fine as far as I'm concerned. She won't be pleased, you know.'

The phone goes dead.

He turns to face Elizabeth. Her face is flushed and she looks at him in some distress.

'You heard? I must be back for Tuesday. I need to travel back into Cork this morning, to make the boat train in Dublin.'

She looks a little shocked but, recovering, nods.

'I thought you might stay for a few days,' she pauses, 'but as you say…work.'

He hurries on with his explanation.

'I'll drive into Cork now, I should really be on the mid-afternoon train if I want to be in London tomorrow morning.'

'I can travel in with you.'

He hadn't bargained for that. He wants to say no.

'There's really no need. You have so much to do here and you need to rest. I can phone you in Bonn when I get back.'

Elizabeth looks at him with something like anger.

'No. I can travel into Cork with you. I need to go and see Teresa anyway and then face the solicitor. Get the bad news about finances here. Arthur can come and collect me tonight.'

In the car into Cork, he admires the fields again, the glow of later summer and thinks, that in other circumstances he would want to stay and walk with her in all of this beauty. She starts telling Charles of one evening last week, right before Alan died.

'Everyone called him Poor Alan last night. It always amuses me how the dead become instantly beatified, even someone as difficult as

The Churchyard in Farahy Cork August 1952

he was in the last year. God, he was hell.'

Charles touches her arm in sympathy.

'I know. You wrote and told me. By the by, I've torn up all the recent letters, best to forget about his last few months. They didn't sum up the man, you know.'

Elizabeth cries for a few moments, gently, as if in relief and then begins to talk.

'We did have one perfect evening with him, last weekend, you know. It was one of the late nights in August when the summer revives, you know, a long, sultry day and then the light suddenly revive and a breeze gets up and Alan had a brainwave in the early evening. Come on, Bitha, let's drive up into the Ballyhouras and have a late picnic. We had guests, John and Diana's two girls, our god daughters and Alan told the children to get out in a forest clearing, right at the top of the mountain, where there was a strong breeze and the children danced in the breeze, while we had our sandwiches and our flask of sherry in the moonlight and the children chased each other around and laughed.'

Charles smiles.

'Sounds heavenly.'

'It was. Alan at his best, you know. I was thinking about that this morning. Perhaps he knew something was going to happen to him. A last jolly up in the mountain. I like to think so.'

'Perhaps,' Charles ventures.

'He planned a two hundredth anniversary party for the house, in 1977.' She laughed,

'I said, by then Alan, we will be all be long dead.'

He returns his car to the hotel and they walk through Cork City to the nursing home to deliver another suitcase for Teresa. It is an old stone building on one of the terraces near the train station, and a young nun takes the case from her. From behind her, the doctor emerges, clearly waiting for her.

'I can report that our patient had a good night's sleep.'

She introduces Charles and the doctor shakes his hand without comment. Clearly his status is known to all here.

'Can I see her, Doctor?'

'Not for the time being. She needs time to settle in.'

'So she's to stay. That's settled.'

The doctor nods and Elizabeth looks relieved. Charles reminds her that he has a train to catch and she takes his arm and walks down the steps. The day is fine and although he has plenty of time to make the train, he has to restrain himself from hurrying. They make their way to the train station and she walks with him on to the platform. There is still a few minutes to go before the train arrives. She turns to him, her face serious.

'Charles, I will be in New York for the spring teaching. Will you come and join me for a time?'

He frowns.

'I'm not sure that I can. There will be so much to do in Ottawa.'

She stops and her tone changes, anger there for the first time.

'I ask so little of you, Charles. You are leaving so soon. This you can do.'

Ask so little. To have travelled three days and left standing at the back of a graveyard. He feels a rush of anger himself.

'I am a *femme seule* now and I know that I will hate it.'

He says nothing, simply takes her arm and presses it.

The train pulls in and the doors are flung open, people beginning to get in. She takes his arm.

'This is our chance, Charles. We should take it. Look at what happened to Alan.'

He looks at her.

The Churchyard in Farahy Cork August 1952

'What chance do you mean?'
'Our chance? Our future? Alan is gone.'
He stamps out his cigarette, his temper rising.
'If only you had waited!' She cries and he turns.
'To be honest, Bitha, I'm not quite sure why you asked me to come here. I was kept well out of sight in the church and put on whiskey duty in the house....'

She opens her mouth to interrupt him but he puts up his hand to stop her. He can feel his face getting red but keeps going.

'Now, I have to travel another two days to get back to my office and then face a desk full of work. I think this is hardly the least.'

He stops. She watches him closely.

Unwisely, he adds.

'Sylvia warned me not to come.'

It is Elizabeth's turn to grow angry.

'I am not interested in anything that woman has to say.'

At this, Charles turns on his heels and marches on to the train, and as the porter slams the door behind him, he stands swaying as the train begins to leave. He makes his way into his carriage and looks out onto the slowly receding platform. She has gone and he slumps down in his seat, feeling old and tired and beaten.

A Time in Rome
1959

In those first moments, alone in the hotel room in Rome, Elizabeth and Charles leave the living and the dead outside in the corridor. Her dead husband. His living wife. With the world hushed and this room now their entire domain, he lies on the bed, his shoes off, and they talk about the siren years. That's what he calls them. Twenty years ago in London when they first became lovers. At the start of the war when death thickened the air, hovered at every footstep, ready to pounce with the approach of evening. 'Then we must make the most of it. I leave on Sunday too.'

The next day at breakfast, she tells him that she is taking him to see a magic wood. The day is bright, with piercingly clear Roman sun and she tries not to remember that this is a week, a short week. She brings him to the top floor of the museum to show him a painted garden, nearly two thousand years old. The excavated mural, fills an entire room, a magic wood in spring bloom, pale greens and blues, enclosing them with its fresh, newly budded trees and its abundance of bird life. She sits and looks around while Charles reads out the information about the discovery of this room-sized mural, buried deep in the ground, perfectly preserved, an entire basement of an

Empress's villa painted to bring the virgin woods alive at her whim.

'We used to visit rose gardens, now it is painted gardens…a sign of age?'

Later, over lunch, he wonders why such an elaborate garden was painted for an indoor room, at the whim of a powerful woman.

'Why, in a country villa, did she order a garden painted, and then put into her basement? Sheer extravagance.'

'It was the nearest she could ever get to the open country, somewhere to escape.'

'Nonsense,' Charles chides her, handing her coffee. 'She was the most powerful woman in the world. She could go anywhere she pleased.'

'Yes, but do think about it, darling. All of the attendants and the fussing, robes to be chosen, precedence, armed guards summoned. Then, if she did get out, there would be petitioners coming up, dogging her ever step. Madam, a word.'

Charles nodded,

'A woman observed, under surveillance. You may be right. Did you see the rabbit in Livia's garden? They always get in, don't they? How is the work coming along on the kitchen garden in Bowen's Court?'

'Oh, I didn't send the cheque yet. I am in trouble with the revenue.'

Charles looks at her sternly.

'Then sell the wood as I suggested. Russell would buy all that timber. It would clear your debts.'

She shuddered.

'I dare not. All my ancestors would come back and smite me.'

Charles makes a small noise of annoyance.

'They are not magic woods and you are not Livia. Really Elizabeth, you need to make a decision about this. You are almost broke.'

His words annoy her, especially when he calls her Elizabeth in that formal way, but the thought of the money she owes him keeps her quiet. At that moment she looks around and her eyes light on figures coming into the café.

'John! Diana!' A young couple, standing in the doorway of the café look over in surprise. Then, in a moment of recognition, they moved towards her, exclaiming her name in delight.

'Elizabeth!'

They all hug and Charles stands politely waiting for all of the affection to die down.

'What good luck? When did you get here?'

She turns and starts making introductions.

'Charles, I don't think you ever met my neighbours, Diana and John.'

'And cousins,' the young man gently chides her, a smile of affection on his face.

Elizabeth laughs.

'Of course, my wicked grandfather married your poor great-aunt, and made us cousins. I think she died within the year of his bad temper. She's buried in the churchyard, you know, next to my father who never had any patience with her...'

She pauses, as a shadow passes over her face and then plunges in.

'And Alan is there now, of course. I wonder what he thinks of poor cousin Georgiana as a near neighbour.'

The young woman reaches over and strokes Elizabeth's arm silently and she looks back at her gratefully.

'Thank you so much for your kind letters about Alan, it was so sweet of you both, and a tonic at the time.'

The young man steals a glance at Charles, unsure of the tone to take and he smiles back and nods as Elizabeth continues to talk about Alan.

'Yes, we did have thirty good years together, I can be always grateful for that, can't I, Charles?'

She thought. Well, that's true. I am grateful for that, even if he haunts every step I take here in Rome.

'And the house?'

The young woman asks tentatively.

'We are heartbroken to lose you.'

'Nonsense, I'll see out the two hundredth anniversary of the house…Charles was just chiding me about the trees.'

The young man leans in, anxious to reassure her.

Yes, I hear Russell has started cutting them down. And the roof is off....' He stops at a nudge from his wife.

Charles looks at Elizabeth in anger but says nothing. The young couple pick up on this and begin to move.

'Oh, but you must have dinner with us tonight.'

Elizabeth tells them, dreading that they will assent and ruin her precious evening alone with Charles. They take the hint and pretend to look suitably contrite as they tell her they can't.

'We are off on the afternoon train to Naples. Back next Monday.'

Back in the hotel room that night, she sits at her desk and begins to write while Charles reads his reports. Her book is due next week and she is finishing the last chapter.

'Josephine's losing of Napoleon must, though dynastic necessity gave it cause, have been also due to mistakes such as love can make – one might say, such as only love can make. To love makes one less clever.'

She looks over at Charles, who takes off his glasses, rubs his eyes and puts down his papers.

'All done for the night. The affairs of the world can all disappear now.'

She turns to smile at him and for a moment, she wonders at the young American woman from the war and what happened to her. 'Eve, or Eva something.' She thinks. 'She has vanished, long forgotten, but I am still here. I longed for her to die. With so many bombs falling in London, I wanted one to hit her.'

She sits up, the sudden movement startling Charles on the bed, and shakes her head vigorously.

He looks at her quizzically.

'Why didn't you tell me you had sold the wood to Russell?'

His glance is fond but clear-eyed.

She makes a shrug at him but doesn't answer.

She stands up, the sudden movement startling Charles on the bed. Outside the door, the dead and the absent. Alan, Sylvia, Eva. Inside, their world. She moves towards the door, reluctant to leave, and grips the handle.

'She was called Eva.'

He claps his hands.

'Yes, Eva. Now I remember. God, you and your memory. I was right. Nothing escapes you.'

She smiles at him. Nothing does. Especially him. 'Time for dinner. I feel hollow,' she tells him.

On their last day in Rome, she brings him to visit the Keats House on the Spanish Steps, very nearly flattening the mood of their final hours together. It is an April day, with the full Roman spring here, the air clean and fragrant, the streets around their hotel freshly washed by an overnight fall of rain. Her book is finished and she will post the manuscript off at the post office in Termini Station, Charles kissing the parcel for luck.

In the sky above them, huge billowing clouds, the thinnest dancing white, are being hurried on by the strong, caressing breeze. Somehow this makes their day gleam as they walk the few streets from their hotel to the Spanish Steps, free of their heavy winter coats. She had longed to see this museum, but somehow in her months here alone, had found herself always stopping at the door, afraid to face the spectacle of young death alone and in her present frame of mind. Now with Charles here and the beauty of their last day unfolding all around them, she suggests the visit as a way of passing their last morning and he agrees, energised by the sunshine. However this euphoria, this vista of promise, is soon dissipated as they make their way around the Keats House, standing in the small bedroom, witnessing a young life relentlessly pursued by illness. In the small room of the museum, they stand looking at the cases full of mementos, one more heart-breaking than another, while through the open windows, the chatter of the crowds on the Spanish Steps can be heard, life outside made lively by the sunshine and the promise of early summer. Somehow the contrast between the lively voices outside and Keats, his young life cut slowly, cruelly short, dampens their spirits and they stand in the painfully small room in increasing respectful gloom. She reads the account of his death, his quiet acceptance of his fate, his air of resignation and somehow she doubts it. On the threshold of life and of love, he must have burned with rage, Elizabeth thinks.

'It must have been hell for him, in this cramped place.' Charles whispers to her, breaking the silence of the hushed room, the other visitors now gone.

'Days and days of illness in these tiny rooms and all the racket of Rome outside. The fever must have made it seem like a madhouse out there for the poor lad.'

She nods, not trusting herself to speak and then motions him towards the death mask.

'Look. Such a bony, elegant face. Like a beautiful young jockey. Unbearable.'

Charles has moved towards another exhibit and she joins him to read about it. It tells of the last letter from his beloved Fanny, left unopened at his insistence, clasped to his poor exhausted chest day after day unread and then buried with him.

'Why not read it?'

Charles wonders out loud and Elizabeth notices a hint of a tear in his eye.

'I don't understand. How he could resist reading her letter? The curiosity would get me.'

She stands there, thinking, 'I do. I did the very same. That letter you sent, just after you were married. It sat for days on the hall table in Bowen's Court and I couldn't bring myself to open it. It was a torment but a joy. I imagined all sorts of things, your renunciation of her, a return to me, and a confession of your renewed love for me.'

They move towards the door and she wonders about telling him about his unopened letter but thinks better of it, even at this late stage. It would mean a reference to Sylvia, even an indirect one and this is now to be avoided. This precious time in Rome with Charles has been bought at a cost, quite a cost, and one of those costs is the things they cannot talk about, on both sides. She has not told him that, in the three months she has been here in Rome, she made the decision to sell her home, the house belonging to her family for nearly two hundred years. She wrote and told her solicitor to accept an offer from a neighbour, signed all the papers he sent her and instructed him to clear out the house as soon as he could. All of this was all done with surprising speed and efficiency. Now, as a result, she is homeless, with all of the books and furniture sold off in an auction in Cork late last month. For the first time in her life she has money. Her bank account is full and all her debts paid but she has no place to live and no idea where she will be. The thought terrifies her and she wonders if she can manage to say goodbye to Charles today without telling him. This is something she can say in a letter, at a distance. For now, the day is still theirs, not over yet. Their time in Rome, dearly bought.

A Time in Rome 1959

Depleted, they make their way out of the museum and stand in the spring sunlight, at a loss, the promise of the day shaded by the remorseless spectacle of young death. No longer young themselves, youth has a kind of shimmering enchantment for them, and the death of the young poet shakes them both. In late middle age, forgotten are all of the doubts and fears of youth and instead there is a kind of glamour in remembering the endless possibilities, the vista of so many lives ahead, so many corners to turn. The brutal fate that Keats faced much too young, appals Elizabeth and makes her somehow unsettled as to her own compromised, middle-aged life. Days spent together like this with Charles have become fewer and fewer in the last decade. Elizabeth stands there and thinks, I am sixty, widowed, houseless, in love with another woman's husband. That is what my life amounts to and yet and yet…I can't imagine what is ahead but these moments with him are a precious country in which to inhabit. Each time she meets him, she wonders, will this be the last time?

As they stroll away, she tells him what she thinks about the unread letter.

'I suppose by not reading it, it remained the perfect letter for him....'

Charles stops and smiles at her, bending over to listen over the noise of the street. He always pays attention to her opinion, always did. That is one of the things that makes him so attractive to her, even twenty years on.

'What do you mean?'

'You see, any real letter would fall short of his imaginings, don't you think?'

Charles grunts and looks unconvinced. She goes on.

'Even she can't have remembered what was in it. We will never know. It was buried with him. Much the best thing to do with it. It remained unspoilt.'

The Last Day at Bowen's Court

He stops and smiles at her.

'I dare say you are right but that was nothing like a jolly for us, was it, on our last day here? Poor old Keats, what a dismal end. We need a good lunch after that.'

He points towards a restaurant near the hotel they both like. Sitting at the table, waiting for him as he makes a call to his office, she sips her drink and thinks. Her time in Rome is over, her book finished and all of her teaching completed. Later that day, Charles will take the fast train north to meet his wife in Paris. They have arranged to travel to Termini station together in the later afternoon. Then, an hour later, she will take her night train to Milan. Milan will be the first part of her slow journey overland to London. She is refusing to think about the days and weeks of dislocation ahead, the vagrancy of her life now that her house is gone. Soon she must decide on a future and on a home, but she cannot think of that now, only of their last few moments together. This is my real home, she thinks, and my time with Charles. It has always been my real home, apart from my writing, ever since we met twenty years ago. If I am to be honest, and I can't be honest with him, of all people, then he is the only person I want to be with. Everyone else is like a shade or a shadow to me, now that Alan is gone.

As he takes his seat, his work done, Charles shivers a little and then remarks, 'We spend our lives in hotel rooms and railway stations. This is what it must be like to be a commercial traveller.'

'And graveyards,' she reminds him.

The previous day, a fine April day, she suggested a long walk to clear her head before the train journey and they made their way to the Protestant Cemetery to see the Keats grave. The day was dazzling bright but as soon as they entered the Cemetery, the cypress trees cut them off from the sun and the underlying chill of the April day returned and the whole place seemed in a kind of perpetual dusk.

A Time in Rome 1959

'There seems always to be a breeze here, even in high summer,' she told him. 'I've been here time and time again in the past few months and I do love it. I sometimes think that breeze is the dead here, sighing and lamenting for home. Much as I love Rome, I don't want to be buried here. I can't think that any of them did.'

She thought about the graveyard in Farahy and wonders if she still owns it or has any claim on it. She must write to her solicitor and find out. She couldn't bear to see it again and she must pay someone to keep the graves tidy. She must ask Arthur to recommend someone. He is in London now, working on the wards and she can visit him there on her return. He was angry with her about Teresa, telling her that she should go and seen her in the convent more often but it only upset Teresa to see her, insisting that she needed to return to Bowen's Court with her, that Alan was waiting for his dinner. In the end Elizabeth stopped visiting her and kept paying the bills and phoning the doctor when she needed to find out how she was. A bout of flu swept through the nursing home early in the New Year, and Teresa succumbed, peacefully according to the letter from the matron of the nursing home. This letter had come to Elizabeth in her first week here in Rome, in early February and she walked the streets in a kind of haze of mourning, crying a little, thinking of Teresa all through her childhood, the times in the kitchen, the smell of the onions for the soup at lunch that always made her eyes sting and the handful of raisins Teresa gave her to console her. Walking through the Protestant Cemetery, Elizabeth wondered if her decision to sell was due to Teresa's death.

She led Charles into the old part of the Cemetery, away from the crowded graves, into the sun again and they stood at Keats' grave, daisies and wild anemones flowering, all around them cats wander, climbing down from the ancient pyramid. Elizabeth walked him away from the grave and towards an old isolated headstone, solid and blocky. Here, the wind blew fragments of seeds around them and cats slunk by, this clearly being their domain, reluctant to engage, roaming freely amongst the dead.

'Look. I found this last time I was here.'

Charles read the inscription and Elizabeth watched him as he read. Two young girls, sisters, buried here in the 1830s. From County Waterford. Moore Park. The Miss Moores. Helen dead in Rome at eighteen and then Isabella, aged twenty nine, three months later.

'Did you know about this?'

'No, I found it by accident, Can you imagine my surprise. I know the house! Moore Park. The family still live there. I was brought there as a child for Christmas parties. I never imagined I would find neighbours here, and right next to Keats.'

Charles read the inscription again.

'How did they die? It doesn't say.'

'Yes I did wonder. The younger Helen died first. Maybe she caught Roman fever, all that malaria, like poor Daisy Miller.'

'And what about the older one? Three months later.'

'Worn out by the fever perhaps and from nursing her, perhaps? Such a tragedy.'

'Like Keats. All of these people much too young to die.'

'Yes. Maybe more of a tragedy for these girls. We do have his poems, at least. We have nothing of these two girls, buried so far away from home.'

'I hope they were pretty and keep him good company.'

'If Joseph Severn allows them near. He was very possessive, wasn't he?'

That was yesterday and now, on their final day, as they order lunch, Charles suggests champagne to lift the gloom of the morning. In the street, as they leave the restaurant, he turns to kiss her, and his embrace lingers, a clear prelude to love. This surprises her as they make their way back to the bedroom. Most of their packing is done and the suitcases brought down by the porter but they still have time and, in the emptied hotel room, he takes her in his arms and kisses her. It is as if the years have fallen away and they are young again, and back in London in those first days of frantic lovemaking. As he undresses her, it is clear that her body delights him as much as it did in those early days, despite the toll of the years both on their bodies and faces. In the quiet hotel room, all stilled by the hush of mid-afternoon and those at lunch or siesta, it is if they have the world to themselves.

His hands move under her clothes and lightly touch her. It seems as if they are making love as they haven't done in years. She wonders at this, and at the urgency of his kisses and the intensity of his pleasure but surrenders to it. Afterwards, on the tangled bed, as he sleeps, Elizabeth tries not to think, this may be the last time we make love, for months or indeed for ever. She longs for a cigarette but doesn't want to disturb Charles as he sleeps. She looks around the room, her home for the last three months, now to be left forever. Her bags all packed away, the afternoon hush, the closeness of his body, and the scents of their bodies, so familiar to her. His face in sleep and without his glasses looks so much younger, unlined carefree and she can still see the young man she knew in London. She wonders about her nights ahead and knows that the time spent with Charles in this room will sustain her, the near miracle of them still being together after all these years.

They sleep for an hour or so and then Charles, looking at the clock, reminds her that they must begin prepare to leave. They dress and comb over the room for the last few items to pack.

'I won't miss this eiderdown. The roses always rasped against my cheek,' she tells him.

He picks up the manuscript.

'All done?'

She nods and then sighs.

'Yes…as to what the publisher will make of it, I really don't know. The ending is wrong.'

'Did Livia's garden make the cut?'

'Yes. I am too fond of her not to let her in.'

He picks up his case and helps her on with her coat and then opens the bedroom door and steps out into the corridor.

'One last check. You go down.'

Something make her want to stay for a moment or two alone in the room and on the pretext of checking the bathroom, she walks around the room, now bereft of all of her possessions. She hadn't realised how much these three months had made the room seep into her consciousness now that she was about to leave it. The last few hours with Charles still filled the room but were soon to vanish and the room become someone else's. Their temporary occupation dissipated forever, and all of her defences here in Rome gone, her books stacked up on the writing table, the postcard of Livia's garden she had wedged into the mirror. All of the small markers of her time there are now dismantled and the room about to become bland again, anonymous, merging back into the multitude of rooms in this hotel, reclaimed for the hotel. At first a prison, it had become her refuge and with Charles even more than that, and now it was dissolving back into nothingness again.

They descend and pay the bills and she hands over her keys. It suddenly strikes her that she has no key to a home anywhere. It feels curious, at once liberating and freeing yet somehow desolate as well. She had posted back her keys to Bowen's Court to her solicitor in Cork, and from the safety and comfort of her Roman hotel room, with Charles expected to come and stay with her, somehow the full implications of relinquishing her keys had not occurred to her. She had no front door to open, like the door in the flat in Clarence Terrace which she pushed open while running up the steps, her London life always something of a whirl with her.

She watches as her luggage is packed into a taxi. This will happen again and again over the next few weeks and it wearies her to think of the hours of travel ahead. She wishes she and Charles could walk back upstairs to the hotel bedroom, shut the world out and stay there. She thinks of Angela's cottage in Oxford, offered for the next month and she decides to cancel it and find somewhere else instead. Anywhere she has been before is out. Aunt Myra wants her to come and live with her in Dublin. A bend back to her childhood, now a sixty year old orphan again, her adolescence prolonged into old age. No, not Dublin, not London, not Oxford. She only knows where she cannot be. Hythe is the only option. Back to her mother, her darling.

They arrive at Termini much earlier than planned. An hour looms ahead before Charles' train must leave, another hour again before she leaves and she doesn't want to spend it in the train station. Charles suggests they go outside the station into the sunshine. She leaves her luggage with the porter and they walk out into the elegant space of the main hall and out into the sunshine. She glances back up at Termini admiringly and he nods agreement.

'You are not supposed to say it, but I do like the architecture of the Italian Fascists. Even in their worst moments, Italians can never achieve anything but elegance.'

They settle down to smoke and drink coffee. Now that he is here, he relaxes and smiles at her.

'So what are your plans now?'

She was dreading this, keeping her movements as vague as possible.

'Two nights in Milan and then off to London. Angela wants me in Oxford by the end of the month, I'm to house sit for her in May and I can do the proofs there, if they get them back to me on time. I'm not sure what it will read like.'

'And when are you due back in Bowen's Court? Can I come and visit in the late summer. I will be back in London for August and I long to see it in the full harvest glory.'

She sips her coffee and thinks, so now I must face this. He has never asked to visit before. It has always been at her express invitation or even cajoling. Now that it is too late, he invites himself. Has he sensed something or did someone write from Ireland? She had sworn Angela to secrecy.

'That would be marvellous…,' she pauses, 'normally.'

She pauses and sips her coffee. He raises his eyebrows. He doesn't know. This will make it even more difficult.

'Normally?'

'Well yes. As and from last Monday, I am no longer the owner of Bowen's Court. I've gone and done it before I was arrested for debt.'

He still looks puzzled.

'I've sold it. To one of the neighbours.'

'Sold.' He looks horrified. He moves around in his chair, almost as if he is planning to get up. She feels herself flushing and getting uncomfortable.

'Don't look at me like that. My ancestors are already haunting me and I can only imagine what my father would say.'

'Oh Bitha. What have you done? And why didn't you tell me?'

'I had no choice. Since Alan went, there's been no money. His pension was halved. And the rates. Crippling. And going up year after year.'

He shakes his head in disbelief.

'But you can't have sold it. It would take months. And what about all the contents.'

'Auction. Last month in Cork City. I did rather well, I think.'

At this, he sits up.

'An auction house in Cork…all those books and the silver. Good God, Elizabeth, what were you thinking of? They should have gone through a London auction house at least. You must have gotten a pittance. A fraction of what it was all worth.'

She begins to squirm, remembering the sense of relief when she had made the decision, the enormous weight of the old house taken off her shoulders.

He shakes his head again,

'What were you thinking?'

She can see he is genuinely upset. Partly pleased that she has made him feel so strongly, she is also jealous of the strength of his feelings towards the house.

'This is so easy for you, Charles. I was struggling to keep the house going.'

She speaks up, a little sharper this time.

'I was thinking of ending my agony, that's what. I am a single woman, and had to make all these decisions myself.'

Something of the enormity begins to strike her as she tell him this but she suppresses it and keeps looking at him right in the eyes.'

'The house. Gone.'

She says nothing, sips her coffee and then,

'You had your chance.'

'When?'

'After Alan's death. In Cork. You walked away. That was our chance, Charles.'

He goes silent but she can see his face working, shock and anger.

'The paintings. The lady with the spaniel.'

'I've put those in storage with Aunt Myra.'

'Aunt Myra. She knows?'

Her aunt was very voluble in her protests, enlisting male cousins to write to Elizabeth and try and stop her. Because of that, Elizabeth decided to hurry and told the Cork solicitor to sell as quickly as possible.

'Besides the house is saved now. The new owner will live there, he has a fine family of children.'

Charles looks at her a little pityingly.

'I sincerely doubt that. The trees are what he is after. Worth twice the price he paid, I suspect. If you can't pay the rates, why should he?'

Charles stands up and throws some coins on the table and turns to leave. His eyes are full of tears.

'Oh how could you? I suppose this is your revenge.'

She sits for a while in the café, unsure if she is pleased or sad that she has hurt him and then slowly gathers herself to follow him. He has walked briskly ahead into the station and for a moment she thinks he is gone but checking the noticeboard, she sees his train is still waiting to go. She hurries to his platform and sees him, standing with the porter, directing his luggage to be loaded onto the train. The train waits, regarding her, she fancies with a kind of arrogant indifference, braced with anticipation. She pauses and watches Charles stand in a shaft of light in the railway station, unaware of her eyes on him. For a moment, he is the young man she fell in love with twenty years ago. Her vision blurred by the fall of light, she thinks, as she thought then, My Darling, My Darling, My Darling. Then she moves forward and he turns and takes her in his arms, to the sound of the train beginning to rattle, the first moment of his journey away from her.

Afterwards. She sits down in a café and takes out the manuscript of her book. In pencil, she writes on the final page, below her neatly typed words, 'My Darling, My Darling, My Darling. Here we have no abiding city.'

Canada

Elizabeth! Are you there? I wake up suddenly in this dark bedroom, in the darkest part of the night, and find myself sitting up and calling out your name. It's as if you are there, just out of reach. But are you? For a moment I believe that I can catch the hint of your perfume, or the echo of your voice but the truth is that I am calling out to an empty bedroom, the vastness of the night-time around me still and indifferent. When I touch my face, to my surprise, my cheeks, my raddled cheeks, are wet with tears. Whatever trace of you I imagined is now dissolved much too quickly.

I sit up and think. 'So…I am still alive…' and wonder if I should feel grateful. I look around. The room is dim, with a sliver of dull orange from the streetlights along the edge of the curtain. What time is it? Three. Four in the morning? No need to check the clock. It is always the darkest time of night when you come, or when I think you are back. Night after night, this happens. Then nothing. I turn on the bedside light and begin this letter to you, this letter to a dead woman. I write to you, lying here, waiting for a sleep that never returns and then I will tear this letter up. Oh, such an endless wait. I watch for the first red tinge of dawn to start licking the edges of the window, announcing another day. Another day I do not want. My useless, fossilised life. Why am I not dead yet? In the next room my wife sleeps. At least I presume she sleeps. Sylvia is ill herself. Although some years younger than me, she waits patiently for a more certain death. She has been told she has less than a year. Her patience and courage astound me, as it always has. I have been so cruel to her. Once I left one of Elizabeth's letters out for her to read. A passionate letter. To punish Sylvia for not being Elizabeth. And yet Sylvia stays here and takes care of me. She may be gone soon but no one can tell me how long I am sentenced to wake in the night and dream of you and my last day at Bowen's Court while I wait for the dawn. I hope it is soon. I could not bear to see her buried. Not another grave.

No one told me that my mind and heart would stay young while my body has turned into that of a shrunken old man. That's the worst part of being old. I look in the mirror and I see young eyes pleading, trapped in an old face. Desire is still raging through me. And dreams. Dreams of you and of your house. Your four-poster bed, so high, one could see directly out the windows. The bronze corn rippling in the wind, demented rooks crossing the half moon. Gone. You were lucky. You died before old age caught you in its cruel grip.

Once I dreamt of a row of your books on a shelf before me. In the dream, I stood there thinking, if I read them all, then I will find you. But each book was blank. Or torn, or flawed. Was I the flaw in your story?

You were stronger, although weaker when you were in thrall to me. Stronger because you had the weapon of your writing.

Once, at the very end, as you lay dying, I asked you why we had lasted so long. To the outside world, we were a brief wartime affair, a fling, lingering on against all odds until I found myself at your deathbed thirty years after we met. You had lost your voice at that point and so you wrote your answer on a piece of paper. A line from Proust. 'The whole art of living is to make use of the individuals through whom we suffer.' I was shocked but I couldn't discount the truth of these few words, written by a dying woman. Was that my function? To help make your books better. To make you suffer and to serve your writing. Well, now, you are the ghost, *the shade from the indeterminate past come back to make me suffer. And I do. Are you pleased now? Is this your revenge?*

Now the first red slivers of dawn creeps across the fringes of the curtain. I lie here and watch the light as it slowly edges along, the intimations of a new day. Soon the birds will start singing, their joyful racket and the creak of the water pipes starting up and all the sounds of a day beginning, a day I don't want to begin. I want to stay in this pause before dawn with you, Elizabeth. This darkness, this borderland world, the only abiding city we have left, like the railway stations and the hotels and the graveyards.

Sylvia watches me. She has grown old too, so quickly in the last few weeks, being ill, and sometimes the pretty young girl she was comes back in my dreams. Other women sometimes. Eva, that American girl, the one you hated. A secretary I worked with once in Paris. Nothing happened but I burned with desire for her. But it is you, mainly. As I first knew you in those siren days in London. In my flat in Whitehall. Discovering the beauty of your body, the unexpected youthfulness of that wonderful body.

I know why you haunt me at the moment, like Cathy outside the dying Heathcliff's bedroom. That letter, two weeks ago, from England. My old friend Clarissa has died. Her daughter is selling her house in Kent and clearing out all the books. On an obscure bookshelf, buried under some dictionaries, the eagle-eyed London bookseller they employed found a copy of The Heat of the Day *First Edition and signed by the writer. Your written dedication. 'My Darling, My Darling, My Darling. We have walked a country together.' The daughter, a kind soul, went to the trouble of tracking me down and sent it on the Canadian Embassy in London. She could have sold it for a tidy sum, but she took the time to send it to me, being kind, I suppose. Kindness on her part, a blow to me. It was cruel to get it. I am shocked by my own carelessness. I have no memory of you giving me the book and the thought that I abandoned it somewhere in a house in Kent appals me. How could I have left such a book out of* my hands? Was I such a lout? I showed it to Sylvia and she laughed when she saw it but wouldn't say anything more then. 'What are the chances?' she muttered and then left the table to be ill.

With a few whiskies, I began to read again and, oh Elizabeth, you demon, how you wrote our time together during the war! The roses in Regent's Park are as vivid to me as the fir trees outside in the snow, the trees I have known since I was a child. This was our book and it was the magic that bound me to you for the rest of our lives, even if I betrayed us, our country, and the country we walked in together, just as your hero Robert sold out to the Germans. But you always forgave me. You needed me and my cruelty to write. I told you early on that I was a crook with women and you said it was how I used my surplus cleverness. I did squirm.

In something of a panic last week, I went into my study and took out all of your letters and mine. Kept in boxes and unread for years. These last few days, I've been reading mine with shame and yours with a kind of terror. I call you a witch in one letter and you were. Your book, our book, was a magic spell that you wove and so were your letters. I envied you your skills and your power. That's how you kept me. Some of your letters, about my other women, your problems with Alan, your cries for more time with me, I felt like destroying them. I even had a fire set in the room. But I couldn't. Some latent concept of loyalty, I suppose. I wish I could erase some of my own part but that is too late. I will keep my diaries as they are. You told me to burn all your letters. I can't. I won't. Is that why you have come back to haunt me?

All those letters and those phone calls. Long distance. Meeting in Rome and in London when I could break free. Once you flew to Paris to have lunch with me. Just for the day. I had breakfast with Syl, lunch with you and then dinner again with Syl. The precious times in North Cork after Alan died, when I could play at being master of the house. Then the house gone. Over three months. You did it without telling me, all *done hurriedly in some auction house in Cork, while you were far away. Generations of Bowen lives abruptly dismantled, the house stripped, the dead ghosts evicted into the fields without warning and no last goodbye for me. Within a year, as a final indignity, the house was demolished. A clean end, you called it. For you, perhaps, hiding in your hotel room in Rome. But not for me. A cruel end.*

Then Hythe. Where your mother is buried. Your final house. When you told me, just after our time in Rome, that you were buying a house in Hythe, I was surprised. But you came to love it there, the Kent landscape, the place you had been happy with your mother and I came to love it too.

Then, all of sudden, without warning, the next loss. Your voice, that light charming voice and your stammer that you used to such effect. A letter came from you to say that you couldn't phone me anymore that your voice was gone and the doctor said it wasn't coming back. I couldn't bear not hearing you and so I came over. I took leave from work, indefinite time off, and came over to Hythe. Sylvia at the airport in Canada, her face like thunder. 'Don't expect me to be here when you get back?' But she was.

You met me at the door, all smiles and keeping the show on the road but you looked ghastly. I couldn't hide the horror in my first look at you. Those last days in Hythe, as you grew weaker, the struggle to breathe, the horror of your illness. No voice. As if your stammer had won and strangled all your words. Every day, you wrote on a pad and I talked. You asked, did I remember the first time we met? Our old game. I did. That christening in Kent. You standing in the church porch. Your air of seeing everything. Romney Marsh from the Library window. Spoken like a true Englishwoman. And then you said, 'Except I'm Irish'.

One day I walked down with you to see your mother's grave, as you asked me, to bring some flowers. You were weak but kept a firm grip on my arm and the cold air must have hurt your chest and throat but you were determined and kept a scarf firmly wrapped around your face. You stood there and looked down and I know now, as I didn't realise then, that you were saying a final goodbye to her and to Hythe. I wondered if this was where you wanted to be buried. I had forgotten the draw of Noblesse Oblige in North Cork. You knew what was happening. You were preparing for the end. When I got you back to the house and insisted you lie on the sofa while I got your pills, you handed me a poem you had written for me. It embarrassed me terribly. But I read it and thanked you. I still have it. On my night stand, tucked into an old writing case. I read it all the time now.

By night-time that day, you looked so much worse and clearly in pain and then I found you had being going to the local doctor all along, I insisted on bringing you to London the next day. I phoned ahead and got us to a specialist, a huge favour from an old pal. You went in alone and, very soon, surprisingly soon, back out you came. A note... Lung cancer. They were pretty sure. Advanced. A matter of days. I had waited outside in the cold on Harley Street and when you came out with the bad news, you got me to light you a cigarette. The die is cast, you shrugged and seemed to say, why not a cigarette now? We walked towards Regent's Park in the December sun but, at the last minute, you shook your head and instead we got a taxi to the hospital. I found that you had brought a night bag from Hythe. I suppose you knew.

Then the hospital in London. A phone call from your Aunt Myra, impossibly alive in her nineties. 'Charles. You must bring her back to Dublin. We can take care of her here.'

But you wanted to stay where you were. I sat by your hospital bed all that week. That's all it took in the end. A week. Not being able to speak, your face became more beautiful. You said no more treatment, just painkillers and morphine. At the end, we drank champagne in the morning and you wrote on a piece of paper. 'I need reassurance.' When I *took your hand, you nodded as if to say exactly that.*

That day, Angela arrived to share the bedside vigil with me. It was very near the end, and we three were together and you asked us to describe Bowen's Court for you. You smiled as Angela talked about the scent of the roses on the porch and the sound of your voice, Darling, w...w...w... welcome...and only Angela could have risked such a wicked, accurate imitation of your voice. In that hospital room, we were all back in North Cork in the lost house. I described the lady with the spaniel and the sight of the rooks as they flew over the autumn fields at dusk, circling in the endless blue sky. I remembered the brash silver of the moon over them, the fire of dusk along the fir plantation, the darkness creeping up the lawn towards the porch, the clink of ice in our gin and tonics. You listened and held our hands and cried with happiness, your eyes filled with the blue of the autumn skies over North Cork. That was your last day. I went out to phone Sylvia and when I got back, you had slipped away.

When you first gave it to me, I hated your poem. Now I treasure it, and the smudge of ink and the tiny print of tobacco where you touched the paper. Also the sky aflame, just like the sky over Bowen's Court.

Unmastered all my mortal fantasy. Was I that? Now you are mine. And I cannot master you. You have mastered me.

The night you died, I went back out and phoned Sylvia again to tell her. I said, 'Elizabeth is free at last.' She told me how sorry she was for Elizabeth's long agony, and I said I was glad that she was now released from it. Sylvia said, 'Yes, poor Elizabeth. She's free, at least.' Later when I got back to Canada, I asked her what she meant. Sylvia said, without any anger, just a kind of sad resignation, 'We will never be free of her, Charles. I'll never be free of her and neither will you.' She was right, of course.

I went to your funeral. We brought you up the avenue to the church in Bowen's Court late at night, and they had torchlight to see you on your way up that narrow, muddy path to the graveyard. The morning of your funeral, it snowed. It never snows in North Cork, as everyone there kept saying but it did. January and the church was bitterly cold, the winter flowers on your coffin, the first narcissus, the snow on my coat. Aunt Myra, at ninety, still as hale as ever, led the procession out into the graveyard in her wheelchair, wreathed in furs. She peered down into the grave and taking my hand, drew me down to whisper.

'This is wrong. I am still alive and I am burying Bitha.' She shook her head in disbelief. 'I saw her mother into a grave and her father and now her. I held her the day she was born.'

Her grip on my hand tightened.

'Oh, Charles, I long for death, and I dread it. You cannot comprehend.'

I do now, Aunt Myra. I do now.

Arthur, a middle-aged man, the local doctor, grey hair, carried your coffin with his two tall sons. As your coffin slid into the ground, I lost control. Her father and Alan next to you and I had no rights. They already had your name on the gravestone and they didn't even mention that you were a writer. A wife first and then a daughter. I wanted to cry at your grave but something, like your hand on my shoulder, made me breathe calm and watch your coffin go into the grave and remain tearless. I thought. At least she will never get to be old. Even with her voice gone, she was still young.

I left as soon as I could. Arthur took care of me, the boy still somewhere in the man's strong face. Would I like to see the house, well, the site where the house was? The steps were still intact. Snowdrops already out along the avenue. 'No, thank you, dear chap,' I told him. 'Just pop me back into Cork.' The snow on the fields, more beautiful than I had ever seen them. I closed my eyes and pretended to sleep. Not daring to look at the fields as we drove back to Cork City, knowing I would never return. It was the last time there. He had tears in his eyes at the station. Apologised. 'I've known her since I was a boy. She taught me how to drive.' We both *laughed at that. You know what a terrible driver you were, darling. 'The worst driver in Farahy,' Arthur said. 'The worst in the whole County Cork,' I replied.*

I never went back to Cork. My last day at Bowen's Court. Except, all the time, here in my mind's eye, whether I want to or not. I want to be buried there not here, not in Canada.

I hated what happened then. Angela and Richard taking possession of all of your things in the house in Hythe, drinking all the wine I brought for you and then thinking themselves so kind as to offer me something from the house, anything I wanted. I declined. For the first time since I had met you, it occurred to me that I should have married you. You were right. That's what you said in Cork train station after Alan's death. That was our chance. Our last chance.

Angela told me that she brought you to see Bowen's Court on your last visit home to Ireland. The house was gone at that point. Demolished. She said you looked like you had witnessed your own execution. Angela said goodbye to me at the station.

'Really, you were so good to Elizabeth. I thought you two would be just a wartime fling but you really stuck to her. Thank you for all your kindness to her.'

She shook my hand. I was so angry. How dare she?

Here we had no abiding city.

Now the room is full of that golden russet light we get first thing on these wintry mornings. I hear Sylvia moving about in her room. Soon the maid will be here, to start breakfast, and then the nurse will call in to fuss about my pills and my blood pressure medicine and give Sylvia her pain killers. I will get up presently and put on my dressing gown and stand and watch the sun come up through the pines and think about early mornings in Bowen's Court. As real to me as the scene outside this window. Elizabeth, you haven't taken that away from me. Each room is in my mind's eye and I live in them. Always I am there, walking up that stairs or sitting in the Library, or lying in the bed in the Blue Room. I walk the rooms of Bowen's Court in my mind and I am happy. No last day there. I am still there.

I envied you the private world where you wrote, where nothing could touch you, your refuge. Now this twilight world is the only place where we can meet. I have a life I want to leave, but ahead there is a darkness waiting for me, where we will not meet.

No abiding city for us. You always knew that.

I stand up and I summon you. The living apparition I long for.

Elizabeth, if you ever thought that you loved me the best, now you have your revenge.

Eibhear Walshe